The Undiscovered Beauty of Genesis

The Undiscovered Beauty of Genesis

A Story of Learning About and
Achieving Identity with
One's Higher *Self*

Peter Kucera

To order additional copies of this book, contact:
Xlibris Corporation
1-888-795-4274
www.Xlibris.com
Orders@Xlibris.com
36876

PART 1

THE SUPERFICIAL EXISTENCE

❖ *Chapter One* ❖

The river nearby with all the crayfish, the brown-spotted yellow-winged dragonflies drenched in dew, Little Bluestem, Goldenrod, Blazing Star Blanket, the Bebb Willow, the Paper Birch, the Red-osier Dogwood, Yellow Warbler, Red Eyed Vireo, the Rock Dove, the Swallows, the grass, the Sky . . . everything around Doug's house was perfect.

The thought never crossed his mind that he would ever be without all of it, that he could even be distanced for a short period of time, or that he wouldn't even want to be a part of it. Unanticipated fortuitous events, however, arising in life may distance a person. Being a part of the human race provides isolation as a screen of shame separating oneself from the world.

Life is beautiful. Doug was able to rejoice in all that it had to offer. He was filled with a regnant but humble energy—nothing could stop him. He wasn't out to hurt anyone, but he lived to his full potential. This was the reality that would be waiting for him. Could he attain it with the impasses that were bestowed in front of this goal?

Doug's life would prove to be difficult, but as with many difficulties comes enlightenment. Many unexpected events came as a shock to him. He never wanted to be an accomplice to murder, but he thought that fitting in with friends like Anthony, Dirk, Big Pete, Raymond, and Slick Willy would prove to avoid the coming of eventual and inevitable loneliness. It would all have been better if he had never even met them. Luke's kidnapping stuck him strongly as well. Even though he was never very close to him, he felt the pain that this abduction brought through the grief his father expressed. As for his adjustment to HYTRE675F that was required after his father's encounter with death at the MMI, he couldn't bear the thought that he would be separated from Old One Eye or his beautiful house near Kingston, New York. The lack of fresh air and sunlight was enough for him to go crazy.

The strength and inner determination that has stayed with him brought him face to face with Andrew. After clearing his mind and traveling to infinity, which was possessed by the light years of darkness and isolation he had traversed, he gained insight into the inevitable decision he had to make between Andrew and himself, and the future of love on Earth.

*   *   *

Doug was confused. The uneasiness was prevalent in his mind and body, but at the same time he felt a certain comfort surrounding him.

He didn't know what to think about his experience. He was confused about his life even more now than ever before. Sitting in the field surrounded by the beautiful environment he thought about what had happened last night. The sun in the sky appeared quite beautiful to him now, and he realized that this attraction was the result of his experience.

He admired all the nature around him; from the small flowers hidden, like the unappreciated beauty of a painting, between the grasses to the ever-present hills that he could call his backyard. Out of all these hills, Hunter Mountain was the most dominant and the most alluring. Its body seemed to jump out of the earth seeking a heavenly peace. The very height that it reached was a sign of its conviction to display and attain beauty. He couldn't place the magnificence of the environment on any one thing. Instead, it was the beauty of each individual element in the environment that produced the resulting feeling of warmth: the thick grass, the pine trees giving a sensation of freshness, clouds, and the occasional passing of a bird. He saw a ladybug on the ground, and felt a strange connection to it. He picked it up, and after studying it meticulously for a while, threw it up into the air. His attention was then brought back to the gorgeous milieu. Just looking at this tranquil scene was enough to feel completely rejuvenated. He was a very lucky young man because not too many people in those days were able to capture the greatness in their surroundings.

Doug stayed outside for a good four hours transfixed by the beauty, walking through what he felt to be heaven. In the past he had never given much thought to the little unimportant things in life. Now, he saw everything. He saw insects crawling on a leaf, and observed them with the utmost interest. He never got tired. He felt like he could do this forever. He returned to reality when he heard his mother calling him for lunch.

His mother was in her forties, and fit the traditional picture of a concerned parent. She wore reading glasses, and her hair, which was starting to lose its original luster to the gray hue that was creeping up, was being colored red. Doug always loved his mother, and indeed this stemmed from the fact that she was always there for him when he needed her most. Whenever he needed something she was willing to give him her motherly support. Sometimes this love was too great for him, and he took it for granted. She never faltered though. Difficult times would only allow her to show him more loving attention.

His father cared just as much for him, but he never showed it as much. This was a result of his employment. Doug knew that his father's aloofness was at times a result of his difficult work. His love was behind a curtain that could be revealed if it were truly needed.

He was lying down at the moment his mother called him, and he got up reluctantly. He wished he could stay there all day. The truth was that he wasn't even hungry. He got home, jumped over One Eye (who was sleeping), and already in the doorway he could smell the aromas from the food she had prepared.

"Ma I'm not really hungry today. I wish that you wouldn't always make so much food. You know that I always leave something."

While his mother was still preparing the salad on the counter, she frowned, and said jokingly, "You know, I believe that you don't like my cooking. That's it isn't it. You poor boy, degraded to eating home made food." She paused to check on the potatoes that, by now, were just about done. Sarcastically she added, "It doesn't get worse than this. After all you never know what concoction I may serve you."

Doug didn't say anything. Instead he turned on the virtual viewer screen (VVS) to see what was new. While he waited, his father suddenly came into the room.

He was into his fifties, but he appeared younger. Most of the time he took good care of himself and tried to eat healthily whenever he could. The refrigerator was often filled with his bottles of vitamins, and drugs that claimed to be the miracles that bring back one's youth. He tried anything to look, and mainly feel better. His whole family told him, countless of times, that it was the addiction to pills which would do him in eventually. He wouldn't listen though, and whenever something new came on the market, he would jump at it, as if it were the last morsel of hope left on the planet.

He had a mustache which made helped lift years of experience off his face since it didn't have any traces of gray in it. His thick dark brown hair looked the same and it didn't show any signs of baldness.

He put his bag down, dropping his papers on the table, and began complaining about what he just went through.

"You wouldn't believe how arrogant some people are. They just don't care about helping anyone nowadays. When I went into the cruiser shop today, they all treated me like I wasn't even there. The bastards obviously don't know who I am. I could get them all fired if really wanted to. They said they would get to my cruiser on Tuesday. The nerve of them!"

"Please, Alan, you're always complaining. You know, your blood pressure wouldn't be that high if you just learned how to deal with people a little bit better." Doug's mother always said something like this. She always looked on the positive side of things. In fact, it was her preeminent quality. She continued,

"Do you remember my uncle Russell? He would find something wrong with almost everything he encountered. I believe that his health was the price he had to pay for that. God bless his soul."

Alan was quiet for a while, and then said, "Rob called me today. He said that he is coming home sooner that he expected."

He then sat down sluggishly, and decided to watch the VVS with his son. Everyone ate mostly in silence, and after lunch Doug decided that he should start to work on his school assignments. Before he was able to sit down, his friend Anthony called and wanted to know if he could go with him to a party. "Doug I was just invited to the biggest party from school. Ya wanna to come along."

Anthony was a person who fought for equality the way he liked it to be. In Doug's eyes he was a perfect communist. He was convinced that anything that didn't receive his advice was somehow flawed.

He felt this way not because he needed to impress his friends. For he chose to be friendly to those who indirectly idolized him. One thing that was certain about him was that he never acted as a double face. His beliefs affected and molded those around him and he couldn't care if it was for the better or worse. What he lacked was self awareness to change because he didn't think that he had to change. Indeed, he wouldn't have had it any other way.

"I think that I will pass on this one." Anthony was silent for a second. "Anthony?"

"Yea, I'm here, I just can't believe that I heard you say that. Man, there will be chicks from every school there and you want to pass such a chance."

"I just have a lot of work to do that's all."

"You are such a kiss ass, you know that."

"Anthony, what are you talking about?"

"I'm talking about a party with girls. That is what I'm saying. And I hear you saying that you have other things to do on a Saturday night. I just see that there is nothin' that you won't do for a teacher. This is ridiculous, I'm going by myself."

"I'm sorry about this, maybe next time."

"Yea, whatever, bye."

Those words stayed with Doug a long time that day. He tried to convince himself that he was doing the right thing, but somehow he didn't feel that he was. He tried to do his work, but he just couldn't concentrate on anything. "What's wrong with me" he thought? "I must be the only kid who wouldn't go through with something like this."

He has always been a little bit on the shyer side, and ever since he could remember, he didn't like it. He has tried very much to change into people that he was not. Maybe that was why he had friends like Anthony, whom he believed would veer him in the right direction.

These weren't his true friends though which he later learned. Who would have thought that trying to bring a present to a sick boy, named Jared who supposedly had the flue for a few weeks, could significantly alter his life? It was a kind gesture, and the way that he got rewarded was with something much more drastic than a slap in the face. At least he still had the people he trusted: his parents, Rob, Bradley, and Susi. His altered life, unavoidably, brought him into a new existence.

It was night by the time he finished his narrative draft for school. He still wasn't pleased with it, and decided to attempt a revision the next day. For some reason, he was feeling exceptionally drained today, and he didn't exactly know why. He decided that the best course of action would be to get some rest.

He didn't sleep though. Instead he tried to meditate.

He got into the practice a couple of years ago when one of his father's friends introduced it to him. He never told any of his own friends about it because he was afraid that they would laugh at him.

When he was a child he was always fascinated with the powers that the mind has over the body. He had done research about it, and came to the conclusion that to live a healthy, and efficient life, one should take some time out of the day for relaxation. When he met his father's friend, he became aware that what he was doing was called meditation. Ever since, he gained more will power to continue his practices.

He found that it had deeper implications than simply calming the body. It also allowed him to do better in school. He got to the point when he could accelerate the healing of minor wounds, and could get rid of headaches at will.

Last night Doug was sitting on his usual piano bench, facing the country before him when he closed his eyes, and began to execute his daily meditation. Something happened. Something beyond words. He went deep within his subconscious mind—so deep that that was all he was focused on. Suddenly he felt a dynamic force present in him. This had never happened before, and it was exhilarating. He was in a state of happiness and felt very secure as if there were nothing in the world that could hurt him. This wasn't all that happened, though. He also had the feeling that his mind was like air and that it could transcend the body in which it was stuck. He could feel the separation very distinctively. This understanding of his Self, gave him the close feeling of intimacy with nature this morning.

Doug's mother thought it was nice her son has found something, such as the practice of meditation, which occupied his mind, but at the same time she didn't want to focus to much on it. It could, after all, lead a person to insanity, she thought.

Alan was a skeptic. He never actually believed any of this. He was the business man type, who never let himself be influenced by others. His very friend who introduced meditation to his son was always considered a fool in his eyes.

As for Doug, he wanted to help his family get used to his practice so that they all could share a common interest. Since he believed he had advanced to an even higher level of the mind, it became harder for him to keep this to himself.

Unfortunately, that is what he did. He didn't want to appear too enthusiastic.

He decided that he would tell his parents about everything at the right time. This experience seemed to him as if he were traveling to infinity, going on never ending voyages, through endless barriers only to be interrupted by the sporadic false sense of reality.

❖ *Chapter Two* ❖

Individualism seeks and crawls just like a meandering vine which seemingly grows out randomly over a forest's surface. While appearing to grow at a leisurely pace in reality every inch of new growth, fostered by the abundant generosity of the superficial semblance of its environment, hungers with an extreme, almost intolerable, understanding of its instinctual urges of survival for the ground and stability which would provide the most sound conditions for further growth.

Concerning individuality, the development of a person's self-expression and identity is a slow process. A person gradually learns how he wishes to define himself. While encountering feelings and passions associated with an identity, one develops a hunger. This hunger is comparably related to the degree of expression that the individual allows himself to show.

Doug got all his feelings from the creeping realization that no one had the right to control him. He was getting in touch with the inward life which question, but which also opposed the conforming outer existence. Since his development was in its early stages, he was mentally torn between the two concepts. His feelings dictated one side of his being while his environment gave him completely different impressions. He was more balanced to the inward life because he received an exultation from his individuality. The more he felt the power of feelings, the more he desired to rely on them and express them. When he later heard Herbert, he knew that for the first time he was truly ready to listen—to experience something different. Herbert's words aroused passions within Doug's soul. These emotions came forth and slowly intensified because he was following his congruence with life.

As the vine crawls into darkness, so individuality directs itself, unknowingly, away from the direction of favorable existence. Recognition is all that is needed . . . . Once sensory perception of environment or its counterpart in the self (a questioning consciousness filled with a new and glorious bright awareness) decides to alter its actuality by redirecting its growth, the vine crawls back into the sunlit conditions. The same is true of the self for once it becomes aware that it isn't expressing itself to its fullest potential then the individuality that it contains, and that is contained by it, is open to the purest form of expression.

The existence of darkness is an ever-present danger. A vine pursuing darkness with bleached and shrinking leaves in hope of finding life giving sunlight (fulfillment) across this barrier of self-destruction might never find its way out. This causes the appearance of the leaves to turn the color of the ground they rest on while eventually becoming a part of it.

For individuality, this darkness and self-destruction happens because of an unfulfilled expression. Doug had learned to listen to himself and ascertain the identity of his life. He had gotten discouraged and troubled when he had thought about others taking away this freedom.

If others were in control of his actions he didn't have the complete expression that he needed. So he voluntarily went into the darkness in order to preserve the person he wanted to become. He was only fooling himself.

As his self matured, he began to feel the underlying truth of a more powerful individualistic existence. The problem arose as to how he should expose this existence to himself—avoiding its containment. A greater belief would have shown that there was no containment—only peace.

Doug had his whole life to learn.

❖ *Chapter Three* ❖

Reality begins to change for Alan. He sees his desk, then the bomb shelter, he sees the picture of his family, the tears in the eyes of friends at a funeral. He wishes it would go away, then he begs and commands it to do so. He shuts his eyes to make it go away, but it doesn't. It can't disappear into the darkness. If only he could tear the thoughts out of his head. If only they were tangible and controllable.

The news came on only a few minutes after the sound, and he saw sections of New York City in ruins. Close to ground zero, there was nothing except what appeared to be miles of a very large junkyard. The huge fires were creating an umbrella of smoke above the city that would last for weeks, blocking out the sun. A few hours later, the people in the news said that the foreign bomb, targeted towards the city, had been accidentally discharged, but later no one seemed to believe that story. The Pentagon had followed the story, analyzing the trajectory of the missile and eventually stated that the only way it could have gotten so close to the city without detection was that it must have been the result of some new cloaking device. They never figured it out, though. It produced the destruction equivalent to an A bomb, but thank God that it didn't emit the radiation of one.

It was one of the biggest disasters in human history. This attack wasn't ignored, but people afterwards certainly wished that it had been. Soon after the explosion, there were a number of conflicts in foreign countries involving investigators. A couple of murders, faceless to the public, occurred which brought out even more hatred between nations. Hardly any people supporting amity in the government were found, but those few that did were clearly outnumbered.

Everything was in ruins, and this disorder led to aggression. Soldiers were sent via the commands of the United Nation to hold the peace wherever possible. This wasn't the best move because foreign soil couldn't stand the idea of being watched. Eventually, there was a conflict between the troops that resulted in war.

Luckily, there were only three incidents in which the military used nuclear bombs, because in this period of history, humans could have destroyed their planet if they hadn't exercised the necessary caution. The Russians who had lost fifteen thousand troops in the first year released the first nuclear warhead. It hit the United States in Washington D.C. which eliminated two branches of the government making its defense weaker. Following this, there were many attacks mostly using missiles that destroyed many major cities. The production of military equipment was up, and the whole country tried to help end the war just as it had during World War II. Many people got together to help the innocent victims. It must have been true what people said: it takes a disaster to bring humans closer together. Everybody was involved in some way, and people weren't such strangers to each other. When they passed each other on the street, they seemed to be saying, "I know what you have gone through. I hope that our children will live a better life." The individuality of the nation disappeared, and it was like one big organism working towards a common goal.

As expected, people dropped their indirect sayings to each other after the war ended. Humanity returned to its inherent nature.

*   *   *

On Tuesday, Alan went to work with his wife Elizabeth. They got there late because they had to pick up their other cruiser on the way. They have been late already ten times this month, and today they both seemed to be a little bit on the edge. They swiftly pulled up to the gate and were checked in. Once inside they tried to quickly get to work. Alan had a very high standing at the aeronautics laboratory. He had been there for eighteen years now, but his boss was the type of person who didn't care about anyone's position. His main goal was to accomplish something. He had a very strict reputation.

Alan looked with despair at all the papers on his desk that he put off reading for another date. He wasn't lazy. The problem was that the management just cut back on the amount of people working on a specific project. He was doing the work of three to four people and he hated it.

Soon his friends, Luke and Sanford, came into his office. Sanford looked notably frazzled, "He's at it again, Alan. He's been bothering Evan and me all week. I'm afraid Andrew wants to see you. He didn't tell me why."

"I hope it isn't bad," said Luke.

"Oh, shit. I knew this was going to happen sooner or later. I just kept avoiding him as much as possible. I really don't want to do this now."

Alan looked at his watch as if he had the power to decide whether he should or should not go.

"Well you better hurry up. I don't think that he wants to wait for you, given the tone that he had with me."

"Allright."

Alan went into his boss's office where he found him turned towards the window. His back faced Alan.

When he walked in, his boss turned around, and gave him a cold stare. It seemed to fit his persona well. He was a short older man who was balding, but didn't seem to be embarrassed by it. Instead of getting treatment like many other people in his position had, he simply cut his remaining hair even shorter. He wore old fashioned spectacles that added to his importance. He always looked well dressed, and he wore the most expensive suits around. He was corpulent, and his short stubby fingers, weighed down substantially by the amount of gold on them, made him appear even more enormous.

When Alan got closer to his desk, and sat down, Andrew tilted his head and looked at him with his spectacles slightly lowered allowing eye contact. This always sent a shiver down Alan's spine and out of all of Andrew's idiosyncrasies he hated this one the most.

Andrew didn't waste any time. Immediately he said, "What the hell do you think you are doing Alan? You are a considered a very industrious worker by a few, but you don't have me fooled. I know that you are a slacker, and one more bad move, and I'll find a replacement for you faster than you can imagine."

Alan looked for a second at his boss and, appearing to agitate him, calmly replied, "I think that you are exaggerating my bad performance. It's true that I came late today which I presume is why you are mad, but I had to get my cruiser fixed."

With a sarcastic smile on his face, his boss shouted, "God, now I am exaggerating am I? You come into my office throwing out excuses into my face believing that I will except them. I am not a fool, Alan, none of this will work on me." He appeared more serious, "What's wrong with you lately? This isn't the first time that you came in late."

"What else do you want me to say?"

"It's not only the tardiness. You have been behind in your work. I think that you are taking advantage of this company. You are lucky to be working with this faction. If we didn't do testing in this area you would have to work in the city like thousands of other workers. We give you a house in the country. Nicely isolated. You like that don't you. I'm sure that you like your salary very much, also." His anger was slowly growing, "We are at the dawn of the twenty second century! Two thousand ninety-eight. Do you even know what this means for us?" He emphasized every word, "TWO, THOUSAND, NINETY-EIGHT. Can you even comprehend its importance? We have many things to accomplish here. You know that technology today is stupendous, and if we don't keep abreast of the new ideas we won't be the number one development company in the country."

"Yea, I know."

His boss was at a loss for words. He just kept looking at Alan. Finally he said, "Now get outta here." As Alan quietly got up he added, "the next time you will be sitting here you will be pleading for your job, and it gives me great satisfaction to know that you won't be able to do anything about it then."

Andrew's behavior bothered Alan, but he knew that he didn't have to worry much because he was liked by Andrew's superiors. Job security gave him the confidence on which he lived.

In front of Alan's office, Alan ran into Luke who said, "I heard what went on in there. Don't take it too hard. He's been tough on many people this week. It is because of this project that has to be completed. Everybody is a little bit nervous."

"Thanks for everything Luke, I appreciate it."

Alan got into his office, and sat down, thinking about what had just happened. He knew that his boss was always somewhat jealous of him. He did after all have a loving family, and he lived in an exquisite area that was very unusual. He just didn't think that Andrew had so much built up hatred. He tried to clear his mind of the uncomfortable encounter, and get back to work.

Somehow he couldn't concentrate, though, and he found himself thinking of the present. He looked out of his office window and saw the city around him.

While seeing it, two thoughts entered his mind almost instantly. One dealt with the admiration of how far human beings have truly come, and the second dealt with the possibility of how this very scene that he was looking at may not have existed today. He might have been hysterical had he received insight into Andrew's future role for humanity.

Rarely, had he ever thought of this. Often, he was just too busy, but his boss opened his eyes a little bit. Even though he believed that his boss was too strict in his approach, he was inwardly grateful that he brought his attention to the things that he took for granted. He realized that even if he had to do the work of three people, it was better than being unemployed, and starving to death, while at the same time watching his family suffer with him.

He became saddened by the notion he had about the existence of the city, because it brought back unwanted memories of what had happened exactly thirty-eight years ago. He remembered it all very clearly now. He was sitting at home on a Sunday night relaxing, when he had heard a distant bang accompanied some time later by a trembling of the house. That was the only sound he had heard that night, but little had he known that it was only the beginning of seven years of what he would call, and what became know as "The Epoch of Pandemonium." It seemed as if the underworld had been brought by the devil himself to the surface of the earth, and it had made the people behave accordingly. He was only twelve years old at the time, but he still wakes up sometimes thinking about it. The last few years he began healing; thinking about the war less, and less.

Alan's memory now became so vivid that the more he tried not to think about it, the more he dwelled on the past. He remembered how his parents would give him most of the food they obtained, and how they would rather starve than see him slightly hungry. It pained him to see them like this, and he did all that he could to make their lives a little bit easier.

Once a missile struck very close to home. In fact it was only a few miles away, and he remembered the fires that spread as a result of this. They just couldn't be controlled. His father, being disturbed, had built a cellar in their basement which supposedly would have saved their lives had there been an air attack.

They all got to know the cellar very well, Alan almost too well. They spent countless hours there, which became very boring. Occasionally, they strayed outside when they had worked in the factories helping with the military equipment, and collecting their ration stamps.

The major concern for them was that some of the fighter planes might have headed in their direction. If this had happened, retaliation would have been difficult because most of the government was inactive. It was difficult for the army to locate the individual attacks, and when they had, they hadn't know what attack style to execute because of poor leadership. The army lost many planes because of this disorder.

Alan's family was lucky to be living in the Catskills because the area around their house shielded many attacks. Also, the remoteness of the area made it highly unlikely that there would be a full blown attack right above their roof. They had to be cautious. One could never be sure.

It had been difficult for everybody, but they all managed somehow. Alan's parents worried about his safety, more than he himself had. He hadn't really understood the magnitude of the danger he had been a part of. Often, he would have asked his parent questions which had made them feel uncomfortable.

"Mommy when are we going to live like normal people again?"

"Honey, we have to live like this for only a short time. It isn't really too bad." She added "Don't worry about anything. We will be fine."

Too bad that her consolations hadn't worked on herself.

"But why are we living here?"

Alan's father looked at him. His eyes were warm, and filled with compassion. His deep voice always soothed him to sleep when he was little. He seemed to speak with a keen understanding of everything,

"Please Alan, be patient it isn't easy for us. There is a war going on. A . . . conflict or argument between people which has to be fixed, and as soon as we fix these problems, we can go back to work, and you," he said with a smile, "you will have to go back to school. You have to be strong son because now we need you the most." He paused adding "You will always be my little soldier, and we both love you very much." Alan finally saw the seriousness of the situation which forever would be a part of him.

Alan always remembered those moments very clearly. He remembered the sincerity on his father's face. When Alan became older he was able to admire his openness, and his determination to help his family in any situation. They had occasional conflicts, but Alan tried to listen to him much. He loved his father, but today he regrets not saying it enough to him. He will eternally remember their relationship.

Indeed he loved his father very much, and he loved spending time with him outdoors. This love was expressed by both of them in the joint appreciation of the stars which served as the middlemen somehow intricately involved with happiness.

It's a shame that the fires destroyed much of the area. He remembered the times when he would go with his father for long hikes. Sometimes they camped out together scrupulously studying the stars with his father's telescope. Alan didn't remember much about this since he was quite young, but he did remember that he father treasured that telescope very much. It was in the family for many years now. His father could spend hours simply looking at the night sky. He taught him all about the constellations, and queried his knowledge by asking him whether he could find them such as the location of Cassiopeia, next to Cepheus. Eventually, Alan knew them all: Corona, Hercules, Lyra, Scorpius, Aquila . . . .

His father got into the hobby when even his father introduced it to him. The two often read books designated to the subject of stars. On the weekends at night they would plot the moving skies and keep a journal to record these celestial positions. Alan remembered when his grandfather had passed away. All that he has of his memory today is that telescope.

The hobby continued with Doug. Alan was glad that the boy's interests were sparked the moment he saw the craters on the moon. They watched the stars with more technology available than ever. They bought an even bigger telescope which they mounted outside. It came with a small dome, and resembled a miniature observatory. They also bought all the software possible for following the mysteries of the universe on their home computer. It was an old an aging hobby, but if the worst thing it did was remind him of the old days, then Alan thought of himself as a proud and dull man. By teaching Doug, what he learned from his father, a part of his dad has stayed alive in Alan's memory.

Alan later would be closer than he could appreciate to the stars he had observed. He wouldn't see them in the glory that he had before. There was no need for it. Before, the glory was a celebration, a rejoicing in the appreciation of the unknown. In this different reality, where hope meant nothing to the wrong person, he became immiscible with the stars with which he so easily used to attain homogeneity.

If he could have understood then the meaning of his coming departure he would have destroyed the telescope out of rage for seeing the stars meant that many people might have to suffer.

After the seven long years had passed and had taken many lives with them and had provided much destruction, the war finally ended. Everyone cheered for the bright future of the county, and mourned the deaths of the people trying to defend it. The war ended because people realized that there weren't many strategically located areas left to destroy. They had all fell victims to the struggle for power.

President Fletcher signed many peace treaties, and the United Nations was back in control. People said that there will not be another war for many years to come, because the effects from this one will forever be present to remind people how foolishly they have behaved. Treaties and promises promoting false hopes were all the people lived for. These were the instruments in which the trust of many lives had been placed, and for which others were willingly ready to die. They knew that nothing was certain, but they still rejoiced in numbers over the vagueness which told the leaders to continue their promotion of the apocryphal challenges. It had been their job to satisfy the people. Peace resulted from this mutual symbiosis.

Reality begins to change for Alan. He sees his desk, then the bomb shelter, he sees the picture of his family, the tears in the eyes of friends at a funeral. He wishes it would go away, then he begs and commands it to do so. He shuts his eyes to make it go away, but it doesn't. It can't disappear into the darkness. If only he could tear the thoughts out of his head. If only they were tangible and controllable.

Alan was still looking out his window when he decided that he should get to work. It was getting late, and for once, in a long time, he felt a strong urge to please his boss doing whatever was necessary. He would even work late into the night so that he could finish the protocols. After some thought, he decided that this would be the best thing to do. He called his wife telling her that he will be home late asking her to pick him up around ten o'clock. When he got home he didn't complain about his day at all, instead he kissed his wife, and felt a strong appreciation for the bed he was sleeping in.

Something clicked in his mind. Like a madman he did work for no apparent reason. He didn't have to please anyone, but fear provoked him. Fear, the initiator, was behind the provocation of many incidents. It wrongly tranquilized thought which he didn't feel like controlling.

In that strange realm of consciousness between sleep and wakefulness he wondered why he spent so much time in the past, and future. Rarely did his thought process occupy the present. The mental injuries he had incurred in the past always haunted his present actions. Now he realized that only for a brief moment. He knew that to rid his life of regret, loneliness, shame, guilt, and hatred, he had to forgive everyone including himself. He wanted to feel peace, but he knew that it came about too painfully. The moment of truth and guiding awareness had been hidden only to be replaced with resistance; a resistance that made sure his hopes would remain hidden.

❖ *Chapter Four* ❖

Mysterious lights were behind him. Their invoking fear reminded him of the world he knew so little about. He could pretend. He could think that he conquered his life, but the beams told him a different story. No one is safe from the unpredictable world no matter how confident that person thinks he or she is.

He had seen these lights before. They were a normal sight. Every day they would be around him, but these followed him strangely, awkwardly. He felt uncomfortable by their closeness. More discomfort arrived as he further questioned the purpose for guiding the light, and making it so obvious. He was almost certain that this wasn't normal.

So he tested his hypothesis. He turned the corner, it did the same. He made a few more turns all with little effect. The cruiser was still behind him. He was being followed.

* * *

The weekend came sooner than Alan thought it would. He woke up late as usual, but his wife woke up at the same time she normally would as if she were going to work. "It will be a nice change to have him over," said Liz. "I haven't spoken with him for ages now. I hope that his new marriage is going well."

"Yea, he said that he was happy. In fact, he just came back from a short trip to Florida."

"Good for him, it's about time that he starts living a little."

Alan walked over to the stove and started to help his wife with preparing the meal. "The last I spoke with him he said that he was truly living life, and that now nothing bothers him anymore."

Alan remembered that he has to pick up his new files at work. As soon as he put on his coat, Liz exclaimed, "Where do you think you are going? We have to get everything ready."

"Please Liz, I am just going to go to work to pick up a few things. I will be back soon."

"I am not going to do this all by myself as I usually do. You are going to help me this time."

"Why do you always make a fuss over special occasions like this? Luke won't care if everything isn't fancy. You know that." He was already out the door when he screamed back, "Give me about an hour."

Doug woke up at about ten thirty.

He hated having company. It wasn't that he disliked talking with adults from his parents work, sure that was part of it, but he simply felt that he could be doing better things with his time instead of wasting hours talking about nothing.

The extreme opposite wasn't for him either. He didn't like to spend hours alone procrastinating. He got easily bored.

Sullenly he walked down the stairs, and immediately his mother found something for him to do. She kept him busy with what he thought were petty things for the rest of the morning.

It was a little bit after three o'clock, and Liz passed back and forth, waiting, while at the same time fidgeting helplessly with diminutive objects. Doug told her many times to relax, but he knew, as well as she did, that his mother would always strive for perfection, and she wouldn't rest until she felt that she had accomplished something. It was a strange behavior and Doug felt sorry for her. He tried to tell her many times that he felt fine, or that he didn't need anything, but she wouldn't accept those answers. He had heard of other mothers that wouldn't have cared if their children even existed. Mostly, when he was alone was he able to realize how lucky he was. When she was around he told her how he felt, but he could never get his grateful feelings out into the open very eloquently. It was the motherly instinct he hated and loved at the same time.

Finally, after waiting half an hour more, Luke finally tapped genteelly on the front door. Doug was calm until now, but there was something about that tapping that made him furious. He couldn't accept the idea that someone could arrive whenever they wanted to. He wanted to go straight to the door and tell him that his mother worked very hard for everything, and that he could at least have the decency to arrive on time.

Of course, he knew that he was out of line, he knew that he was thinking thoughts that were irrational, but to him they were only thoughts. He would never even consider acting on them. That's the way he was. It seemed as if thinking things like this would somehow alleviate the tension in the situation.

As Doug opened the door, he put on the mask that he so often created at will when he was faced with a public conflict that he didn't quite know how to handle. He wanted to hide. When he acted the way society expected him to, he surrendered his personality and identity to their expectations.

He was still upset inside. Maybe it had nothing to do with his mother. Maybe it was because he had held something against Luke. He didn't know what to think about it.

When he looked at his company, his heart instantly changed, and he felt a sudden rush of happiness spread through him. He was speechless for a few moments The change was so quick that it caught him off guard and demoted him down to a mumbling mess.

Luke brought with him his daughter, and she was beautiful. In fact, she was the most beautiful girl he had ever seen in his whole life. She had long dark hair, and hands as delicate as freshly fallen snow. Her breasts roundly filled her blouse. When she smiled, Doug had the same warm feeling as someone who had just won a small fortune in the lottery. Her legs appeared smooth, and as they took her inside, she moved as if an air of elegance constantly hovered about her.

Doug didn't know much about Luke, but now he wished that he did. All he knew was that he became divorced, and married someone who was half his age. The third person standing at the door must have been his new wife. Looking at this other person now, he thought that perhaps she might be a little older than he had thought. He knew her name was Ellen. He, also, knew that he had a daughter, but he never envisioned anyone like the girl he saw.

Liz timed her entrance from the hallway just right so that she could greet them all face to face. She apologized for the lack of her husband's presence. Doug thought that she looked worried when she mentioned this, and he understood why.

Where could his father be? He would call if he knew that he would be late.

"So Luke how have you been doing. I haven't spoken with you in a long time."

"I manage. You remember my daughter, Susi."

"Oh Yes, why the last time I saw you, you weren't any taller than this chair. You certainly have grown." Liz, putting their coats away, asked, "How old are you now?"

"I'm seventeen"

"My, time certainly does fly right on by."

"Trust me I wish that she could still be that little child that I brought from the hospital seventeen years ago," Luke said. "By the way, your son doesn't look like the little toddler I once used to see running around in here."

"No, he's eighteen now. They sure grow up quickly, don't they."

Time was misunderstood by all of them. It expressed itself and was often characterized by many in terms of age, height, maturity, love, and the ability to be able to follow one's feelings. This is all that could be measured of time. A clock shows the effects it leaves behind just as a trail of smoke is visually left behind by a plane that no longer exists. Time can't be grasped without first grasping the unity in which it is forever and timelessly imbedded. For now Doug normally existed with and therefore expressed the influences he had been exposed to since childhood.

It takes isolation in the unity to redirect the misguided stream of consciousness. For now, convention was good enough.

"Liz, you haven't met my new wife yet. This is Ellen. She also works down at NAST."

NAST (National Advancement of Space Technology) was a subsidiary organization resulting from extensive expansion of NAB (National Aeronautics Bureau). About forty years ago, right before the beginning of the war, drastic cuts in funds from the government were made. There was the general attitude that humankind needed to reach the zenith of its living on earth. When word got around that a tremendous amount of the citizens' taxes was needed to support a space program, which was believed to be created only for the amusement of scientist, the president of NAB was forced to abort the project, and later shut down NAB for good.

Directly after the war, there was a sudden influx of capital at the country's disposal, and there were, yet again, new doors open for space technology. The organization reopened its research departments, but only in its subsidiary branch: NAST. From then on, NAST has grown prodigiously with little mention of its former creator NAB which has transferred all its research to the former. It has achieved its glory in the spotlight when it discovered life on Mars. Even though this consisted only of microorganisms, it demonstrated to the government the necessity of further research.

Since NAST was so big and well known, it didn't come as a surprise to Liz, that Ellen worked in the same company.

"Nice to meet you. Which department do you work in?"

"I started in the new engineering section . . ." In the middle of Ellen's sentence, Alan rushed in, sweating. He quickly shut the door behind him, and kept looked outside to see if anyone was there.

Liz looked on in terror, "Alan, what in heavens name have you been doing? You had me worried sick. I didn't hear anything from you for hours."

Alan leaned against the door panting, "I've been followed from the plant."

"God! Come on let us sit down. I'll get you some water."

As soon as the tension in the room was abated, Luke asked, "Did they attack you?"

"No I was lucky, though I believe that they wanted to hurt me. I picked up the last of my files from the office, and as I was going back, I noticed that a gray cruiser followed me for at least five miles. I felt that something wasn't right, so I pulled off into a side street. It followed, and for a moment I lost sight of it. I think that it turned its lights off. I suddenly was hit from the side, and ran off the road. I thank God that nothing happened to the engine. I shut off my lights, also, and sped into the opposite direction. Then I made a few more turns just to lose them. I waited by the lake until now."

Liz looked horrified, "You're very fortunate. I dread to think about what they would have done to you if they caught you."

Everybody was quiet for a moment. Then Alan said, "The damage to the cruiser is pretty severe. I was surprised that she was able to take me this far."

"Goddamnit Alan, forget the cruiser. It can be replaced. Just be happy that these goons didn't do the same thing to you that they did to Aaron."

Liz asked, "What do you think they wanted?"

Without hesitation Luke took up a responsibility to answer.

"The same thing they were after when they attacked Aaron. Not too many people know about what happened to him because NAST is trying to cover it up. They can't help it when the media gets a hold of it, but they try to control it as much as they can."

"What?"

"I really shouldn't be saying this, but if I couldn't trust you, then I really couldn't trust anybody." Luke leaned closer as if he feared somebody was outside. "Last month you all heard about those accidents that happened in sector 44. My friend, Aaron, was among those that got killed. I'm sure that you have heard from many people that the building collapsed because it was a good sixty years old."

"Yea, they mentioned that an investigation was underway."

"Nobody except a handful of people knew that this has been part of a terrorist act. I don't know how much longer they can hide the truth. Especially when their attacks are becoming more frequent."

Alan looked at the friend whom he knew for over twenty years now with a serious face, "What do they want?"

"As you know, we have been working on the new project: V.O.R.T.E.X."

"All that I know is that people from your department have been complaining about the amount of work that they have to finish by November. That whole place is a mess."

"Yes, well, it's worse than that. We are working on a means of getting energy by way of fusion. We have people working day and night on this, and we have almost succeeded. Now it is just a matter of time before, we make a large enough model based on our experiments. We have fulfilled the Lawson condition which as you know is the critical combination of factors allowing fusion to take place. Many fusion laboratories all over the world have gotten a part of this condition, but we have been the first to put it all together. With this breaking technology we could literally power the world."

"Amazing!" Alan looked around the room looking for words. "This could be the breakthrough that we all needed."

"Unfortunately word of this got out, and now others want it. I haven't been told of all the people who are involved, and now I don't think I want to know."

Luke was honestly telling them everything he knew. He hid no facts, and he wasn't afraid to tell them anything. They should have known.

"This is what I heard. Someone told me that they are planning to attack workers until, an agreement is reached between this foreign government and the head of NAST."

"They killed all of those people I told you about, but the leaders of the project had an urge to throw everybody into a building, and claim that the collapse was the result of an explosion. This was all too easy for them. All they lost was an old warehouse. Nobody has found any of the bodies ever since."

Alan was quiet. He sat steadfast taking in everything that was being said. Finally he said, "I can't believe that NAST would do something like this. Once this energy was discovered, the group of scientists should have gone to our government, and get it protected."

"You don't understand Alan, we did that, and our government is trying to hide it more than anybody."

"That makes no sense. Think about the possibilities for improving this country. They could build factories which don't emit pollution into the air. Christ! Most of our boarder states are already flooded. Any more warming of the globe and who knows how are children's children will live. We wouldn't have to worry anymore about fuel, and we could begin focusing our energies on improving the standard of living. The possibilities are endless!"

"Listen, our government fought for the fossil fuel that it has now very hard. They plan that it will last us for another fifty to a hundred years. Do you really think that they would throw all that out the door? They can make money off it, while they use fusion for their own research."

"Are you saying that this is all because of money? America's well being is at stake, and all they can think about is money?"

"That's right. What would happen to all the gas stations, oil reservoirs, and the thousands of people that are employed there? There would be a tremendous loss in profits. All those people that could be helped with this new energy are expendable. What isn't expendable is a life of luxury. As it stands today, the government posses this new knowledge, and it is trying to ward away any negative, in this case foreign, influences."

"I think that the government isn't looking at the situation correctly. With this new energy, we wouldn't be hurting the economy, we would be helping it. Think of the increases in production alone that would decrease the national debt."

Luke shook his head, "Yes all this will happen, but in good time when the remaining fuel is used up. We will have a powerful economy using what we have At the same time we will be using this new technology secretly. You have to also consider the fears that we have."

"What fears?"

"I know that all this might be difficult to understand. Maybe it will help you if you see the whole picture." Luke paused thinking about what he was going to say as if he needed just the right impact. "The economy is one thing, but it isn't the entire reason why there is a massive cover up underway. If the lives of the people who would be affected by fusion were the only concern, then I am convinced that the government wouldn't have so many doubts about introducing it, but they are also currently worried about foreign powers. We may be the only country able to create such colossal amounts of energy now. This is a great advantage we have, but it is likely that if this knowledge is held in the wrong hands, then it could easily be abused. We have to protect it." He took a drink. "I am not so sure that our government can do this, but it is all we have to rely on for now."

Allen didn't know what to say. He just sat enthralled saying that it made perfect sense. Everybody in the room felt the same way. They didn't know how to react because this groundbreaking news was like a sudden earthquake. No one expected it, and when it arrived they all had to accept it if they liked it or not. Ellen seemed to surprise everyone when she broke the silence asking, "What type of material is used for creating this energy? Isn't there a limited supply of it in the world?

Luke began to speak this time more incisively than before. "No. This is something I forgot to mention earlier. Let me first get into the background of what we have been doing. Fusion joins the nuclei of two atoms to form the nucleus of a heavier element. In our first attempts we used hydrogen and other lighter elements. The speeds required for these nuclei to collide were achieved by using a particle accelerator. The fuel that we originally used in fusion experiments consisted of a gaseous mixture of deuterium and tritium, which are two heavy isotopes of hydrogen. We eventually learned that the fusion of one pound of light nuclei produces as much energy as the burning of about nine thousand short tons of coal. This intrigued us, but we had never thought that we would achieve even greater results without using these elements. Our experiments led us to a crucial point in our work. We discovered how to separate electrons from the atoms that matter contains. This can be done with most objects with the exception of those that are extremely dense."

Liz quickly interrupted Luke, "Are you saying that you could release great amounts of energy from simple objects on this coffee table?"

"Yes Einstein pioneered all this over a hundred years ago, and we already created much destruction with it. Now it's time that we put this knowledge to good use."

Alan said, "I wish that more people could know about this. Maybe we could save a few lives if we inform others." He paused. "We are all shitin' in our pants, afraid to lose profits."

"You know that we can't do that. I know this sounds terrible, but it is for the best. Think about it this way. If we try to help a few people, then many more could be killed because there is a risk that information could be stolen. Then many people's lives are in danger of a possible futuristic struggle for power. This can't happen."

Everyone spoke about this well into the night. There were so many issues that this new knowledge brought up.

Alan somehow thought that by discussing them he could make them look less austere, but deep inside he knew that he couldn't do anything about them. Even if he tried, he would only be doing more harm than good. He wished that nothing had been discovered so that humans' true nature would stay hidden in a world of chicanery.

One good thing about this was that now he expected things to happen which previously would have been unexpected for him. Was this a good thing after all? Luke's words just like Andrew's words helped him see that he shouldn't be taking life for granted. Waking up in the morning, going to work and earning money to provide for the family while trying very hard to please everybody day to day—that is all that should be consisted in life. He knew better though. Had he forgotten all that happened thirty-eight years ago? He should know better than most people how difficult it once was. He should know how difficult it is to hear about someone's relative dying as a result of the war. He should know how difficult it is to tear open the wounds that have, almost perfectly, been healed with time, and how they are better left closed. It is just that some things are too apprehensive to constantly think about. Why should he dwell on the past, when he has a lovely home and family for which to care?

At the end of their discussion Luke said that he was going home because the night wore him out. He said that the terrorist, or whoever those people were, probably didn't follow him home, but that he should be careful nonetheless.

As Luke helped his wife with her jacket Alan felt a surge of guilt, "I'm sorry that we didn't have more time so that you could tell us about your trip. Maybe we could get together some other time."

"Sure I would like that. How's your older son doing?"

"Oh . . . a . . . he's doing well. He said that he will be back soon."

"I am looking forward to meeting him again." Luke paused for a moment, and then said, "By the way I want to remind you not to spread anything that I have said here today. You might be surprised how easily this information could be passed on."

"Don't worry Luke, I can see that I'll have to be very careful about what I say anywhere now. I'll tell Doug not to say a word about this in school. Even though I'm sure he would be cautious."

As they continued to chat at the door, Doug spoke with Susi in the living room. Speaking to her was like speaking to a goddess. She was friendly, and Doug liked that she wasn't as haughty as many of the girls in his school were. This is why it was easy being around her. They spoke about school, and their interests.

Doug found out that he has quite a few things in common with her, one of which is yoga. She said that she started when she was about ten years old and was charmed by some of the things that yogis could do with their body, and the rigorous exercises that were required. He would have listened longer, but he remembered that there would be a dance in school next week. Without hesitation he invited her, and for the first time in a long while Doug felt genuinely lighthearted. He couldn't remember the last time he felt so comfortable with a person.

Luke yelled towards the living room for Susi to get ready. He said that he kept everybody up late enough. Before Doug was able to blink he already heard the words "goodnight, and so long" come from Luke's mouth. He didn't mind the late hour at all. In fact, he wished that he could spend all night getting to know Susi.

As they walked out the door, and as Alan shut it, not a single person noticed the eerie silence that was present that night. The earth was resting. It was exorbitant by detaining the vivacious sounds that were normally present. This type of quiet wasn't ever present before. Even the stillness after a storm was different from this. After a long thunderstorm on a summer afternoon, that may have caused much destruction, the silence afterwards didn't resemble death as this silence did. No, it was teeming with life, and all it required was the right person to hear it. The silence of a single tree might otherwise fall on deaf ears. It required a knowledge that transcends material roots that are so important in keeping a tree in place. It required appreciation. Everything after a storm was alive, in contrast to this now dark scene. If somebody had looked at the woods nearby, they would have appeared under the moonlight as if they fitted into a picture that was taken for the sole purpose of capturing a strong semblance of isolation.

❖ *Chapter Five* ❖

Lies. He had tried to help inform them as much as possible, but all he succeeded in doing was to enlarge the circle of benightedness. He filled them with lies—unaware of this seduction originally offered to him. If only he could have known the unimpaired truth. If only he could have done something about it. But knowing doesn't always provide a solution to a matter.

Luke was right about the fusion. NAST has tried many different methods of attaining what they considered almost free energy. They all proved futile. The gigantic establishment has used deuterium and tritium in their fusion laboratories for many decades. It was only temporarily set back by the bloodshed thirty-eight years ago. What they used wasn't unexplored. It was used by many scientists in many countries.

Their original goal was to use the fourth state of matter; a plasma containing deuterium and tritium maintained at a very high temperature and held together long enough for fusion to take place. The way that they held the plasma in place was to use a magnetic bottle: a magnetic field that acted as a container. This technique was called the tokamak. Now the nuclei were able to be confined into a doughnut shape which took care of the container.

There was still the obstacle of how to heat this plasma to a temperature resembling that of the sun's core. This was taken care of by shooting a beam of particles traveling at very high speeds into the plasma. Another approach was to vary the magnetic field which caused an electric current to flow in the plasma, in effect heating it. The density of the plasma had to be given due consideration because if it was incredibly low, only one hundred-thousandth of the density of air, then few nuclei would collide with each other every second, making the process very inefficient. To get a high enough temperature, hold the plasma together for a long enough time, and obtain a high plasma density was the condition properly dubbed by Luke as the Lawson Condition.

Once scientists found out that the fusion energy released is equal to the power needed to maintain the hot plasma strong efforts were underway to secure a correct model. This meant that enough energy was released to sustain the plasma reaction without a need for further heating. A joint agreement was made between the United States, Japan, Russia, and the European Community to work towards an International Thermonuclear Experimental Reactor (ITER).

Its construction went along as planned until it encountered the early developments of the ANTITECH. Nothing but ashes remained. The person who was responsible for this destruction was let into the facility covered with enough dynamite to level three city blocks. It was some sacrifice: his life in return for slowing down the advancement of the science. Things became slow after that. People didn't care about fusion, and they were willing to put all the funding for it towards more rewarding things.

After the war things got heated up again. NAST, and the whole country was aware of the limited natural resources available on earth. People knew that fossil fuels weren't the perfect source of fuel.

The sulfur and nitrogen alone produced the acid rain whose effects were taking their toll on many buildings and forests in the Restricted Regions of the country. These regions showed the most prominent destruction. They resembled acres of desert where once vegetation or civilization used to thrive, but now were reduced to a wasteland. All that was kept there was tons of garbage that degraded at a faster rate than outside these regions. A person could follow the barren insipid land all the way to the horizon in hope of some small glimmering plant, ready to face the far too harsh world, all in vain.

The fuels had their advantages, of course. They were life. They were growth. They helped people eclipse the animal kingdom, and now they were limited in availability by reason of their very usefulness.

No wonder astronomical projects were underway to find something suiting for people to use. They were concerned with the opposite of what Luke was talking about. He had heard rumors about hot fusion, but what NAST had perfected was the age old question about the possibilities of cold fusion. Greed fueled the projects design, and misconception brought about its success.

Pioneered by Martin Fleischmann, and Stanley Pons, cold fusion frequently found itself in the center of heated scientific controversy. The two electrochemists used heavy water (D_2O) which is abundant in natural water sources in an electrolysis experiment. They also used the rare metal palladium which has the unique property of hydrogen absorption.

With the use of a car battery, they hooked up their equipment and placed the negative, and positive electrode in the heavy water solution. They theorized that while the oxygen gas bubbles off at the positive electrode, deuterium nuclei would enter the palladium metal of the negative electrode, and with a large enough voltage the nuclei would be held so close that "quantum tunneling" would allow them to fuse. Such a high level of heat was generated that the scientists assumed that they had found fusion. The good news was that no radiation was present.

All of this happened about one-hundred years ago, but people still couldn't always successfully replicate the experiment until NAST expended millions to effectuate the original techniques. The teams of scientists worked day and night to meet deadlines, and proved that it was all worth it. All it took was a car battery, and two lone scientists.

❖ *Chapter Six* ❖

One Eye was his best companion. They were inseparable.

In instances of haste, love temporarily gives way to hatred only to later restore the power, generated by the unified consciousness, that it uses to suppress evil.

His dog would listen to anything he said, and wouldn't complain. It became more difficult for him to express himself around others who did complain, though. His mother was a perfect example.

How could he tell her? How should he go about saying it? He has tried before, but it was always dismissed as something that was unimportant. He felt it was important though, and he stood by it one hundred percent.

His mother simply wouldn't listen to that garbage. There were continually more important things that had to be done, such as the laundry, shopping, fixing some old piece of furniture, or anything imaginable, just as long as there was no time for what Doug felt was important. On one day it would be fixing up the house, on another it would be the backyard. Doug would hear, "I am not really feeling up to it." The same was true of his father since he seemed to be even more busy than his mother.

At least if people listened. That would be different because then he would be fooled into believing that they cared, which would bring some satisfaction.

Whenever he said anything concerning it, a few moments would be given up only for the purpose of elegantly changing the topic. It didn't seem harmful to him or anybody else. Why was there so much resistance? Doug decided once that the best thing to do was to catch everybody off guard. Unfortunately, this didn't work so well as he planned. The same disheartening results were observed.

Doug had a small sphere in his chest. His whole body was one big orb that he thought would never open even though he relentlessly tried. It had no definite boundaries, but he was more than aware of its presence in everything he did. Awareness, meant that he was consciously preoccupied with some task while his subconscious mind was still on the prowl. Awareness was the supreme eminence of this part of his being.

Some might call it his mind or soul. It could even be considered a small Earth residing inside him; a microcosm of his environment altered by his experiences of it. This sphere stored all his abstract thoughts, and noteworthy experiences. It was undervalued. It began to grow in thickness around the age of ten. The walls of which were constructed of a transparent material that could allow one to easily see outside, but definitely no one could look into it.

This wasn't a problem since no one ever wanted to anyway. All he could do was hold on to it the best that he could, and make sure it was safe. A treasure that couldn't be looked at; shouldn't be looked at.

This treasure was held in place by an underpinning much greater in strength than any material wall could provide: an individual will mutated by the existence of social prejudices. Doug's will was what kept his sphere shut. Unfortunately, he forced himself to do this for fear of the guilt caused by going against convention. When he spoke with someone it would stay shut, building up the power and potency that lay inside it.

"Hey ma, do you want to hear about what happened to me last night while I was in cogitation. I think that it was fascinating." Doug said this with a smile trying to look important. His tone displayed extreme arrogance which appeared to be very whimsical, and funny. He was only fooling around, but the reply that he got wasn't the one that he was seeking.

"Cogitation?"

"That's right I said cogitation. It just means meditation. I read about it somewhere once."

His mother was programming the wall computer while speaking. She smiled without looking at Doug, and said, "You are really something you know that. Where do you find the time to do all this?"

Turning rather serious Doug looked at his mother, "You don't like that fact that I have an interest in something."

"Oh damn! I forgot to shut of the auxiliary power. Your father hates when I do this. I expect that the other circuits are fine." She threw her tools onto the ground in disgust. "I might as well continue. It's too late to do anything about it now. What do you say?"

"It'll be fine ma. We'll just have to deal with any problems, damages, breakdowns, explosions . . ."

"Oh Doug, stop it, I didn't cause the end of the world."

Doug felt that a long time passed while he watched his mother work. "So what do you think about it?"

"About what?"

"About what I have been saying to you about my experiences."

"Right. Well, I don't know much about it. So I can't give you any advice."

"I don't want advice, I want to know if you are even a little bit curious. Aren't you interested?"

Her head was in the wall, and she was grabbing at the emptiness behind her for something. Doug kicked a bundle of wire towards her hand.

"I can show you how to do what I know so far."

"That would be great, but I have to do this before your father gets home." She paused while Doug just looked at her. She looked up at him, "O.K. I'll tell you what I'm going to do. I will talk with my friend Will Simmons. You remember him don't you? He was at the last company picnic, a few years back. He knows a lot about this stuff. Maybe you can speak with him, and ask him any questions that you might have."

Doug left the room to go outside. He was bored. Especially now that he couldn't go anywhere because of the threats employees have been receiving, he had nothing to do. He went for a long walk to think about things. His face lost its dullness when he saw a patch of chamomile in a clearing. It spread from one end of the clearing to the other, and he walked through it slowly.

His urge for mental satisfaction retreated behind the covered protection of the sphere. It had the potential to be enlarged or even destroyed, but now it fell back into itself, only to give way to random thoughts about life. Thoughts, he believed, that were just pondered without the presentation of accompanying actions were useless.

What was better? Was it better to be in the inner city, fighting through the smoke so that one could seek enjoyment with numerous forms of entertainment, and claim to be happy? Or was it better to be alone in this forgotten wonder which gave one a different form of entertainment? Not too many people were able to enjoy such a scene now. They all stayed close to development since it was the provider. Why should one drive many miles a day just to live in one place, and work in another? It would be a waste of time. Especially when the city can provide for *almost* every need imaginable. If it was nature that one was seeking then that wasn't a problem. There were parks in every city for a person to enjoy the benefits of nature, while at the same time live a life of untold misery.

There still were people, of course, who lived in what was once called the suburbs, but these people were in a separate class that they created themselves. They could be considered to be the weaker group since they couldn't survive very well in the new supercities. These people lived in the suburbs because they felt a strong attraction to a part of the old way of life. They refused to give it up.

As Doug walked around his house he dwelt on these issues. At times he even surprised himself, and asked whether it was normal to have these thoughts going into such depths. Shouldn't he be out living life, and enjoying it more instead of just thinking about it?

He walked around the house to his RAVIT that was hovering about two feet off the ground. The RAVIT descended from an ancient model ATV which kids often used before in open areas. There are great differences between the two. The RAVIT can go practically anywhere; even about water. It could out maneuver many of the older recreational vehicles, and it could even become air-born for short periods of time. Doug loved it. He spent hours outside riding it and investigating the countryside. It's appealing characteristic was that it had great fuel efficiency.

He was outside riding for about an hour when he stopped, and decided that he should go for a hike. He hasn't gone hiking since the incident that occurred one year ago. The air was warm and softly tickled his face. It was remarkable that there were droplets of water sporadically falling because the sun was brightly shining giving the impression that there was no darkness whatsoever in the sky. Old One Eye was right by his side, and he followed Doug's every move. A trail led to the top of Hunter Mountain. About halfway up the mountain, Doug found his usual overlook. This was his favorite place to sit. From it he saw the man-made lake that was created a few years back, the tops of some gigantic pines, and the silhouettes of distant pines embraced by rays of sunlight.

The lake, as beautiful as people claimed that it was, seemed out of place for Doug. When he deeply stared at the landscape, it didn't fit into its security. If he had been prompted for a reason he couldn't explain. It was just one of those images that wasn't accompanied by a genuinely jocund emotion.

One Eye was sitting next to him, and while Doug lay with his back on the pliant and downy moss he thought about how much he loved his dog. On weekdays when he and his parents came tired from the outside world One Eye would have the same greeting for them. He would never tire. He would jump all around them wagging his tail in delight of their presence. It was surprising that even if he was ignored by his masters, he still displayed the love he appeared to be saving up all day for that precious moment of addressing his them.

When he was young, One Eye was crippled due to a fight he was in. Only, this fight didn't involve another dog. It involved a person, and the words "What does your father do for a living?"

Doug was exactly eight years old when he first got into trouble with another boy living next to him. It occurred on his birthday. He had a big party, and invited some of his friends from school. Doug decided that he shouldn't think twice about inviting his next door neighbor—Ian, even though he didn't know him very well.

The only problem was that Ian was a very jealous and invidious person. He was envious of Doug's big house, and of everything he possessed. What made things worse was that Ian's father was working for Alan, and the company was going through some mayor changes threatening Ian's family. This wasn't Alan's fault, but Ian being young and susceptible to outside influences that affected him, thought that whenever his father would complain about his job at home, and disparage his coworkers, it was because Alan was making it a living hell for him.

This is the way some adults mitigate events that threaten their lives. They complain about deleterious occurrences in their lives believing that in some way they will alleviate the resulting pain often caused by these occurrences. What happens is that the complaining spreads. It is an illness to other people, agitating them as well, and so is the case concerning Ian.

Ian was not only concerned about his father's job, but he was deathly afraid that his family will have to live on the streets. His mother used to scare him by saying that without a proper education he would starve. This was a very simplistic attitude, but it did serve its purpose well. Ian would do anything just to watch himself and his family succeed.

There was something deeper to his paranoia of failing in life. He had the constant fear that he would be all alone without anyone to take care of him one day. This constantly threatened his mental well-being. At one point he became possessive of his parents and couldn't do anything without them by his side. This condition, later diagnosed by a family physician as obsessive compulsive behavior (OCB) grew progressively worse and worse.

At night the boy would seek asylum in his parents bed just so nothing happens to them at night. Throughout his illness of the mind, his personality fluctuated. One day he would be very irascible, another he would be timid. There came a point when he couldn't function in daily life anymore, and needed counseling due to serious neurotic behavior.

Eventually, though, with treatment he got better and better (he remarkably lost many of the previous symptoms when he realized that his family was paying a large amount of their income for his treatment). Everything was going well for him until the day Doug invited him to his birthday party. Once there he became aquatinted with many people, and began enjoying himself. He loved the outdoors, and once he saw the hiking trails by Doug's domicile he immediately wanted to try them out.

Enjoyment was going to lead to terror very quickly. As it would, it would catch everyone, except the initiator of that hatred, off guard.

Two boys walking up the side of a mountain and enjoying nature. What harm could be present for them in such an environment? There could be bears, they could fall over the side of a precipice, they could be bitten by a snake . . . as should always be anticipated. Doug's mother often cautioned him with the generic statements that are always somehow expected from a mother before he went out into the woods alone: be careful, don't stay out too late, I heard of an increase in tics this year, try to stay away from the tall grasses and shrubs, and so on. Not that Doug ever obeyed anyway, but in the presence of his mother he felt that she deserved enough respect for him at least to listen.

He could have prepared for anything he wanted to that day, but he would have still overlooked the most threatening and abstract thing found in nature: the human mind.

As the two of them began to slowly crawl up the side of the natural traverse, everything was in order. They laughed at similar experiences, and disported. Doug couldn't have known what was about to follow when he casually mentioned, "What does your father do for a living?" Ian was just climbing over a rock when he stopped and lost control of all his body. Since, at the moment, he was holding on to a sapling for balance, he let go due to his disorientation, and fell about ten feet bouncing all the way down the rocky incline.

Doug knew that it wasn't a serious accident, but he rushed to his aid anyway to check if he landed in a bad way and possibly broke any bones. Once he got to him, he shook him for a second or so, after which Ian jumped up turning the rescue into a brawl. Doug, being the lighter, and weaker one, was getting injured pretty quickly. He already had a broken nose, and cuts all over him which slowed him down substantially, while Ian was powered blindly by a history that didn't care about any damage that would be done to his body.

Doug's cries weren't heard by anyone, except his dog that he got two days ago (as an early birthday gift). He was lying by the entrance of the house when he heard a distant cry. He arrived at the scene just in time for Ian to get his small pocketknife opened. He jammed it into the dog's eye. Excluding all the blood present, there wasn't time even for a whimper from the canine. Instead he stumbled off the trail blending in with the leaves as he rolled down the feeble hill.

Doug felt that it was a very clumsy action from him; quite unnatural and deserving pity. Doug believed that under natural conditions animals have an aura cohering of an innate and graceful elegance. Only rarely could such clumsiness as his dog displayed be seen. It would require the viewing of an injured animal or even two animals in battle for one to capture the irregular motion seen on this day.

Doug managed to keep Ian down for a few moments which was just long enough for the injured dog to get back to the top of the hill filled with more anger than a wild swine who has just discerned that her offspring have been menaced. The powerful hound jumped on Ian's back from behind a tree and would have killed him if it hadn't been for Doug, once he found the strength to move, and to still his dog's aggression. By then, Ian couldn't get up by himself. In fact, Ian wasn't ambulatory for one whole week afterwards, and he had markings on his arms and legs that would be around all his life.

What happened inside Ian when he heard the sentence from Doug that triggered his reaction? Opposed to contrary belief, the human mind is unstable and constantly trying to fight off threatening influences despite their eventual infiltration of the mind's defenses.

Sigmund Freud, the psychoanalyst of the nineteenth and twentieth century, understood this well. People like Ian reached a point in their lives when they couldn't deal with the pressures of life. To cope and function properly, the mind tries to protect the organism by a means of self preservation. It suppresses the thoughts that are unpleasant, and in this manner they don't seem to affect the body. This is what Freud's outline of psycho-analysis is all about.

When an individual suppresses an unpleasant memory or thought, he is putting it into the subconscious realm of the mind. It isn't actively troubling the individual, but the horror associated with it comes out in other ways. The individual may, for example, develop another nervous disorder such as some kind of uncontrollable flinching. This behavior alleviates the trauma of holding some thoughts in a different realm of the mind.

Repression could turn into a serious disorder if the repressed material is too strong for the mind's energy to ward off. Then the symptoms become more severe. Among some of the cures, for a person demonstrating these symptoms, are hypnosis and free association. By venting, the malicious or dark thoughts, the individual becomes normal again. These thoughts may be perfectly normal for the person to have, but it is the society that makes them appear to look abnormal.

If a boy, at a very young age, falls in love with his sister or another family member it is considered to be immoral, and right away, Freud stated, that the boy's parents or some public figures will step in to teach the correct behavior. The previous thoughts held in the child's mind become suppressed, and the child begins to feel ashamed. Everybody has a type of neurosis (the symptoms expressed as a result of suppression) since almost everybody has been taught to conform to the rules around him or her as a child.

This all leads to the composition of the mind which is equivocal because man cannot possibly probe deeply enough, yet, to discover secrets of his own complex labyrinth. But theory dictates three separations of the mind: the id, the ego, and the superego. The id consists of the individual's instincts, the superego consists of a parental influence and reminds the person what is correct and what is wrong. The ego is the mediator between the two. It tries to keep the person balanced.

When Ian suddenly went berserk, he was at the point of his ego breaking down, unable to continue exercising control over the body. He was reminded in an instant of all the pain he went through in the past. His superego lost control along with his ego, and all that he could hold close, sheltering him from the circumstances, was his id. He grabbed it and allowed his other self to retract entirely under the jurisdiction of this ID. He was completely savage, without any thought about what his actions could do to himself and others. Was it his fault that he became injured? No it was greed that became the underlying cause of his suffering.

The only explanation lay between the Id, ego, and superego. Psychoanalysis conveniently gave titles and names to the unknown. Mankind tried to make the world a more comforting place by attempting to fight the unknowns of the mind. It fooled itself into conquering a battle that never started.

After Doug became conscious of the time, he looked around, and thought that the sun was belatedly setting. Since the incident during his birthday a few years back, he felt servile towards One Eye. He didn't feel as if he had to be a servant, he wanted to, and willingly enjoyed basking in the thought.

On his way down to the RAVIT, that day, he encountered a pungent odor leading him to a dead squirrel lying on a patch of barren ground. Not being repulsed by it, he carefully looked to see what the cause of death was. A shot right below the mouth, and in the head, left an impassive expression on its face. The rain that fell a few hours ago dried on the squirrel, curling the hair around its mouth into an immutable smile.

❖ *Chapter Seven* ❖

When parents discover a disquietude showing itself all over their boy's face which is pellucidly expressed, what can be done about it except ask a few questions? Is there an underlying reason for the expression, or is it a general mood into which all people occasionally fall. If so, asking about it could only further the unknown tensions already present.

Maybe it was just one of the facts of life that teenagers go through different mood swings. Maybe nothing could be done about it. A person's behavior couldn't truly be understood without the accompaniment of truths.

There could, however, be a danger involved in the youngster's life that remains a concern hidden deep within the minds of his parents. Therefore, a need to act is called upon, and absolutely necessary to authenticate his normalcy, despite any irritation it may cause. These types of instinctual reactions are necessary for his role models to possess.

Doug was sitting quietly inside waiting for the storm to pass while he was thinking about these thoughts. He thought about his parent's decisions, and how they affected his life. He went to get something to eat when he became aware of his drifting mind.

He went to his room and sat down at the new desk that just arrived yesterday. He was lost in contemplation mostly because of ennui rather than interest.

So this is how he would spend his summer: thinking about the past. It didn't appeal to him, but he had no choice. He couldn't find a job anywhere, and his parents convinced him that it would be better if he relaxed and got ready for college in the fall. He could study physics at his own pace, his favorite subject, and pretend that he took a summer course.

He didn't mind being alone, but what bothered him was that he felt useless to his family. He knew that the income was there, and that there was no need for further money, but he still wanted to feel appreciated.

He spent his time meditating, reading, exercising and target shooting in the field he called his backyard. He finally had time to do all the things that he couldn't have done, but, given this opportunity, he hadn't felt like doing them.

He lay next to a cooler feeling detached when his mind began to take control again. It was captivating him for a change. He clearly remembered the milestone in his life before graduation.

Doug was anxious while he waited for his breakfast. He wanted to get out of the house quickly today. His parents asked him whether anything was wrong, seeing the discontent on his face.

Getting no reply was the hardest thing. Naturally, all they could do was to repeat themselves until their point was made. The telecom rang before Doug was able to give out a sharp and painful "NO!".

Just as he left the house he restated some unimportant details that they already knew with some apology in his tone. Pausing at the door, he finally told them that he wasn't feeling very well, but he could still go on the trip as planned. He also mentioned that he would call if he needed anything.

That morning, Doug left the house with an intention that wasn't his own. A few weeks ago, a boy he had never seen was causing trouble for Anthony, Doug's friend. Doug wasn't ever really close to Anthony, but since he didn't have many good dependable friends in school, he was afraid to distance himself from him.

He would have spit in Anthony's face had he known more at the time. He would have gladly distanced himself if he knew that it would avoid possible starvation for him. He needed to be powerful, and alive, not caring if the world dies. Lost alone in the woods without anybody to talk to, seeing three dead bodies (believing there were four), feeling helpless without even his parents to lean on, was what Doug faced. It was appalling.

All of this trouble was indirectly caused by the birth of one boy—Anthony. In actuality, Doug couldn't blame Anthony. Doug's life was shaped by his past insecurity around Anthony.

Anthony had short hair, and it was slicked back. It appeared to be wet from the great amount of hair spray he used. His body was rather small, but he dictated respect in every movement he made. He never lost his cool. Indeed, he based his whole personality on this fact. He even walked a certain way to avoid the clumsiness everyone else shows once in a while. He wore a golden chain that was big enough to be worn by a millionaire, but didn't look odd on him. Due to his slow and precise motions he was on the heavier side and, because of this, the chain looked like it was made for his body.

He wasn't a good friend, though. Occasionally, he would show emotions of friendliness, but these were rare. He was the type of person who didn't care about anybody, and it seemed strange to Doug that this particular personality trait was what made him so popular with others. When he didn't want to speak with anybody he would simply let them know by completely ignoring them. This was his way of dealing with others. He even did it with his parents, who weren't very fond of his superciliousness.

Most of his spare time was spent with his friends from his old school. He often went with them to a local club to shoot pool, which was one of his favorite pastimes. One would always spot a girl around him. There was something which attracted the opposite sex to him the moment he spoke. Doug was more handsome, but the only girl who ever really liked him was Susi. It was the charm he was missing, and this charm was what made him want to spend as much time with Anthony as he could.

Once Doug stepped out of the house, he felt that the sun was welcoming him as it caressed his body. It was pleasant even though it was about ninety degrees outside because he was frozen from the cold air in the house.

Four other boys that he didn't know very well were going along: Slick Willy, Raymond, Big Pete, and Dirk. Doug occasionally talked with them, but he felt that they really didn't like him. Maybe it was because their interests were so different from his own.

Just by their appearance Doug found himself adjudicating them in his mind, and making up sentences for them, thinking that they were felons. Big Pete, and Dirk especially stood out from the crowd looking like hoodlums. He knew that they could be completely different once he gets to know them, but he couldn't help his one-sidedness. He didn't want to know them.

The cruiser came later than he expected. When it pulled to the side of the small road with the ruffians inside it shouting, he ran without even thinking about the impedance that was present as he trampled the dwarfish but copious yellow flowers that covered his lawn.

Whenever Doug had a slow day at home, having nothing to do, he would act completely different. His whole metabolism slowed down as he spent time outside. Under different circumstances he might lie down and read a book occasionally relaxing his eyes by staring at the same flowers.

It was different today. If someone who knew him well was watching him, he would appear as a discursive person who can't stay fixed on a given personality for long. It was the need for excitement that did this to him, and sometimes while alone he would think about whether he needed it. It brought action into his life. It brought excitement and relaxation, but, strangely, it also introduced exhaustion and agitation. Maybe he wouldn't go crazy if he were alone after all.

Doug was going up to Ellenburg near Quebec about one hundred and eighty miles from Hunter. He told his parents that he and the boys were going to celebrate their graduation from high school two months earlier at a party up there. He didn't want to divulge any other information because he knew his parents would worry about his safety. He mentioned that he was excused from school, and that he didn't really have to be present anyway since these last few days he reviewed material that he already learned.

They made it to Clarksville near Albany about forty-five miles from Kingston in about twenty-seven minutes. This is because they traveled one hundred miles an hour on the highways.

Ever since the creation of these cruisers, a proposal was passed with the help of the National Transportation Safety Board which stated an increase in the speed limit. These new cars could never run off the side of the road because censors on the side of the car detected any objects within three feet. Also, the cruise control was so precise that no one had to operate the vehicle while on the highway. Satellites controlled everything.

This made people uneasy. Computer technology was taking over the world, and in the process it was ruining civilization. People, part of the ANTITECH group, fought against many advancements, but in the long run these were inevitable. Kids that grew up during this age couldn't imagine a world without this technology.

Every generation has a group of people that try to expunge new things. Change isn't important. It is feared. If a person listens closely enough he can hear the advancement of civilization. He can hear the cries of righteous and inculpable people who have suffered for no real reason. He can distinguish between the cries of hunger from children in a land with a bounteous amount of people, and the cries from soldiers dying in a war caused by a need to possess a surplus amount of possessions. He could be able to hear all such sounds, but fail to hear the crescendo of devastation that is bound to encompass the future.

The boys walked through the small town of Clarksville to look around and get a bite to eat. The town used to be different in the past, and it had a certain beauty from a distance, but up close one could see the damage and squalid conditions in which people lived. It was obvious there wasn't any money to make the repairs necessary.

The town lost most of its business due to an influx of foreigners. Many immigrants moved there, and others couldn't stand living with them. Anywhere else it wouldn't have mattered, but because this town was so small everyone knew their neighbor. Conflicts between families started, and eventually it turned into a mini ghetto.

Anthony's friends fit right in. They saw an old lady getting into an apartment building that seemed to be missing a whole wall on one side. It must have fallen down years ago. Two of the boys started shouting obscene words at her, while the others interrupted them only with their laughter.

Doug tried to get them to stop, but once he did so all he saw was each separate expressionless face staring at him. He was, as his best friend would say, in a fine pickle.

He didn't want to be the one ostracized on this trip, and mostly here in this ghetto, so to amend his behavior he said that he was hungry, and was going to get some food. They all agreed narrowly averting Doug's individuality.

They spent the whole day in Clarksville by pointing out the most trivial things that they thought deserved it. This was how they wasted their time. Their actions were so unimportant that their minds avoided committing them to memory. If asked about their daily occurrences, they would have been at a loss for words.

They decided to spend the night in a motel they found in the unscathed part of town.

Everyone seemed to be instantly comfortable upon entering the dwelling except Doug. His eye caught the cracks in the wall, and the wretched conditions seen everywhere. As his so called acquaintances, for that is the only word which could have been used for them even though Doug would have wanted otherwise, sat on the couch and watched the VVS. Doug went into the bathroom.

He wasn't feeling well. Maybe it was because he empathized with the crone whom his friends insulted today. She probably thought that he had not only condoned his friends' behavior, but that he had actively partaken in the critiques. He couldn't stand it. Every time he concentrated on the feelings she must have had and clearly grasped her possible emotions, he felt guilty and ashamed of himself.

Of course, maybe he was sick because he was in the presence of people that he couldn't stand. It could have also been the left over caviar that he had for breakfast when his mother wasn't looking, and which he realized was becoming fuzzy only when he saw the bottom of the jar. In any case whatever it was he felt bad. He thought he was going to throw up, and when the others asked him if something was wrong he only replied that he must have come down with the flu. He stayed up most of the night in the bathroom. It suddenly passed him, and he went to sleep on the floor.

It was likely that this temporary affliction was the outcome of all the day's events. In the past Doug's body would react very quickly to a change in his mental awareness. During his first day of school, he couldn't eat anything due to his nervousness, and if he did, he would feel sick to his stomach like on this day. Most children get insecure, but not to this extreme. That's why the cause of this discomfort came from his affiliation with people he didn't really like. It was one thing to go out with them, but quite another to witness and almost be a part of their daily actions.

Doug never thought about why he was sick. He couldn't combine thoughts with his condition. He went over in his mind what he ate not even considering his mental outlook during the day.

They woke him up early in the morning, and said that they better get moving. Slick Willy was the first to get up. He poured himself some water which was anything but clear. It was similar to the carpet; it should have been clear and should have had a natural looking color to it, but instead it was dirtied by a lack of concern, and effort. Willy's way of waking Doug up was to pour a bucket full of this water over his resting head.

The five of them got something to eat, and commenced their journey again. In the cruiser, it seemed to Doug that Raymond had droned on for hours about more trivial things. First he talked about how he lives on the edge, of course he didn't use those words. He wanted his audience to come to that conclusion by themselves. He mentioned how he loves skydiving, and the thrills it gives him. The comment about jumping out of a plane on a bicycle was a little to hard for Doug to swallow. Later he switched the subject to what he and his friends stole two years ago at a local food market.

He really annoyed Doug, and Doug thought that the others felt the same way. As a period of silence came upon them, he thought about changing the subject. At one instant he opened his mouth, but he couldn't convince himself that speaking was the best thing to do right now.

Doug couldn't imagine Raymond opening his mouth again, and he was fairly certain that the others would be quiet also, especially Big Pete. Pete was a strange kid. He rarely spoke, but he hadn't failed yet to catch Doug off guard when he did. Always expecting a timid voice as that of an introvert, Doug heard something quite different. He would be pounded by a voice that presented itself with aplomb. Also, Big Pete didn't speak if he didn't have to which meant that he had no interest in making friends. All of his friends had something in common: they were the ones who befriended him.

Doug heard a word come out of Raymond's mouth. He interrupted him, "I like this cruiser. Whose is it?" Dirk, who was driving, turned around and looked at Doug.

"Oh, look guys he likes it. What a nice compliment. I think what we got is a fucking sissy on our hands. Lets get rid of him." He upbraided him harshly some more, and then laughed, getting applause from everyone except Anthony. He overran the automatic controls, and pulled over to the side of the road. "I don't know where you find some of your friends Anthony, but I sure as hell don't like them."

As he opened the door, Anthony looked at Dirk, who was lost in the excitement of picking on a helpless person, and slapped him in the face. He then shook him coarsely and said, "I know you're just kidding, but try to avoid treating Doug like this. He's been my pal for a while now." After that things returned to the way they were.

Willy, and Pete didn't even care about what was going on around them. They were immersed in the alcohol that they made a part of their lives way to often.

Doug's spell of squeamishness returned. He lay back in his seat and locked up his eyes. He didn't want to look at anyone anymore. His mind meandered, like a dipsomaniac in the streets concealed by the night, to the moment in time when Anthony asked him if he wanted to go on this trip.

Doug just completed what he felt to be a perfect antiquity test. It was concise and he was proud of himself for using the ingenuity that his teachers customarily abetted. While he went to the parking lot to move his illegally parked cruiser, Anthony was just pulling in. "Hey party-goer" he yelled. He invited Doug to go with a few of his friends to a graduation party which, even though it was a bit early, he convinced him, would be festive.

Doug was caught. He knew that he had to respond now or never. He thought for a moment and said to himself, "Why not?" He couldn't think of any reasons to go, but it was enough for him that he also couldn't think of any reasons not to go.

"Great, I will pick you up at your house in the morning in two days." Anthony's enthusiasm tapered off as he continued to speak. "Just make sure that you are on time. I will have a few of my close friends with me, and they would hate it if they had to wait for you."

He understood, and went inside to get lunch. He sat down next to a crowd of kids that he wouldn't normally deem friendly, but his ego played with him, and his superego was nowhere to be found.

"Now I will truly be liked. People are beginning to notice me. All I have to do is to be around them, and I will be accepted." Again, thoughts without actions to prove their beliefs were meaningless.

The truth was that his own friends already accepted him. This wasn't enough for him, though. He had to go further without perceiving the old adage: "One can only be friends with some of the people some of the time, and not all of the people all of the time."

A big kid with a nervous twitch of the eye who appeared to be the main speaker said, "Anthony is so pissed off. This kid, Seth, has been bothering him for weeks, right, so he wants to go over to his house and off the kid. You know what I'm saying. He simply can't stand him. I heard that he's been messin' with his girlfriend also. That would get me pretty fired up. I know that. I couldn't stand it if some fucker had his hands all over my girl. He wants to make it nice and clean. Nothing obvious. Nothing too noticeable, get it."

Someone interrupted him and said "Yea I get it. I get it that you have a big mouth. You sonovabitch. Just shut up from now on. You talk to much."

It turned out that these kids were also Anthony's friends, and they talked about the party.

That was about the end of that. He presented everything nicely on a platter for Doug. The only thing that he didn't know, was where this kid was living, but he figured that he would find out soon enough.

Should he go on this escapade? Can he get out of it now? Why would Anthony want him to go along when he would obviously be with his friends? He didn't know. He also didn't want to pull out now. He postulated that this was all a joke.

After all, Anthony was like the macho Italian type even though he was really the fifth generation of his family born in the United States. He must have loved any energetic attention directed towards him. He probably spread this rumor to boost the admiration among his friends. Doug once got inside information that Anthony accidentally hit a bystander with his old cruiser. When people asked Anthony in school he told them that, this man was one of his archenemies. The person who told this to Doug elegantly finished his story with saying, "He's full of shit. I don't need to have a friend like this."

So Doug's conclusion was that this trip was innocent fun, and that his friend had no ulterior motive which could be proven. For if he wanted to do something he wouldn't have invited him.

It was getting dark, on account of their need to stop in Middle Granville near Lake George for a few paraphernalia. They got to the party one hour late, instantly getting out of the car to socialize. Doug didn't have the same craving. He found a stand with some food, and stood there for a trice. He was without a comforting hand. Without definition. Without a comfortable place where he could belong. He was like the Amerasians, who have both American and Asian decent, and who don't feel attached to any one home. When questioned they might say they belong to both lands, but only inside themselves do they know the veracity of who they are. He was lost in this sense of despair.

He was enervated by the excursion and yet he discovered himself mesmerized by the reflection of the moon on the surface of the pool nearby. Just by looking at it he was a pioneer conquering it without really understanding its essence which could be made clear only by virtue of his deep amalgamation with it.

❖ *Chapter Eight* ❖

Doug felt powerful, and alive. He couldn't care if the world died.

The party gloomily continued well into the night. Doug met a few people that appealed to him, but he couldn't open up to them. His conversations with them were one-sided and it wasn't a wonder to him that they soon excused themselves.

Anthony appeared to be having fun in spite of his nervous preoccupation with his watch, which he regularly checked every few minutes. At roughly a quarter past eight o'clock the five of them, Dirk, Pete, Raymond, Willy, and Anthony got together and startled Doug as they approached him from behind.

They said that they were going to a friend's house who couldn't make it to the party because he caught the flu. They asked him if he would like to come with them, an invitation which Doug declined. He didn't want to stay at a house with people he didn't know. He had it that day and knew that he also didn't want to go anywhere with his so called party-goers.

It was no use. They pried about why he wanted to stay, and it was apparent that he wouldn't get anywhere with them so he consented to go. They left with a different means of transportation than they came in, but Doug didn't say anything.

"Here is his driveway" Dirk said. "We will be right there. Can you just take this up to the house and give it to him and say that you hope he feels better." He handed him a little box, which was covered with exceedingly blue wrapping paper. It was topped off with a flashy bow. They said that they had to go park in a remote location so that they could come in through the back way and surprise him.

Doug was delighted that he could help. His previously ill-tempered mood slowly descended and disappeared into the well recognized pool of naiveness. He visited it often—daily. Whenever he disapproved of himself he swam. Whenever he hated his life he thought a harmless dip couldn't make anything worse. He now felt like basking in the light of genuineness next to the pool. The only problem was that, to find it, he had to overcome his resistance to change. He struggled for a breath of wisdom while submerged in ignorance. From the outside he appeared calm. On the inside he was tearing himself apart. The undercurrent prevented him from rising above the water and he felt shallowly satisfied. His satisfaction came from knowing that he had others around him. Every time that he was hurt in his life by friends or strangers he believed that it was merely a bad break, and that things would soon change. He repudiated evil in the world, or at least evil concerned with his affairs. "It couldn't happen to me" was his covert motto.

He held that he could treat others with as much disrespect as they treated him, when his mother prompted him to change on occasions if she witnessed strangers taking advantage of him. Doug said that he could be different, but whenever he met someone who was likable to him he couldn't find it in him to act differently. He counteracted the person's kindness with a much greater kindness that revealed the vulnerability he shunned.

Call it what you will: be it ignorance, insecurity, self consciousness, instability, or even philanthropy and amiability, what Doug possessed would be a part of him forever. He might have tried to change himself had he disliked what he saw, but it would have been very difficult. He would have only been fooling himself if he thought that he could act completely different. Truth was that will power lasted only so long. When he let his guard down his symptoms of weakness showed again. They were leaking from the source of his being which he didn't think of obstructing.

So when he was asked to carry this beautifully decorated box given to him by people he didn't trust to a person whom he didn't know, his belief about how he should act took over. He disregarded his soul which was communicating with him—a communication that any other person might have listened to in a situation like this—to be aware of the flagrant danger present. He jeopardized his safety because he was recalcitrant to his intuition. He cared more about others than about his existence, and this is what he needed to be conscious of to choose a deviant road in life.

As he walked up to what he thought was an exquisite house, he felt as if he had once lived there. It was beautiful, but in a strange way as if each person had to discover the beauty separately. A fleeting glance in its general direction wouldn't arouse any issues of extravagance. On the contrary, one might be ashamed of its condition with its dense foliage creeping up at its sides, and the meadow grass conquering the potentially spacious property more and more every year at its own leisurely pace. That was it! When he pondered about its looks, he obtained a picture from his mind's eye verifying his emotions. It was because the house was unkempt that it was attractive. Further thought brought nothing. He couldn't answer why.

Standing on the first step looking at his feet he saw the moss encompassing the stone. The moss was quite tall and when he lifted his foot, he found that he had bent it. Upon closer inspection he saw that there was poor drainage in this area, and when it rained the water was forced to stay where it was and to slowly evaporate creating an exceptionally strange plant. The vision confirmed what he remembered reading once: moss is only limited in height by the water level around it.

He loved it, and wished that his front steps at home were just like it. His parents say that he would make a good scientist, but who knows with the attention that he gave to nature he might make a good botanist.

He was lost in amazement when something finally struck him. He couldn't explain it since it came so abruptly, but he felt a panic and then a fright pass through his body. In an instant he began to doubt his companions. The story he heard in the cafeteria about Jared became vivid. He saw Anthony's face. He recreated Jared's face. He now saw his own hands tremble.

He assumed that Anthony wouldn't hurt Jared even if he hated him, but why would he be considerate to him? He knew before anything happened. He threw the box over a lofty embankment near the house into a compost heap.

A few windows cracked. The sounds of birds nearby stopped. The side of the house was burning.

The magnitude of the explosion forced him to the ground driving upon him a temporary loss of orientation. He thought the house had collapsed. The compost didn't look like a heap of anything anymore. It was leveled in a microsecond, and some of the lighter debris was still falling, making the moss he cherished just a minute ago black and obsolete. Other than a cut from the railing, Doug was intact, but he wasn't held in readiness for what was about to come.

Someone opened the front door. His terrified eyes met with Doug's own timorous eyes. They looked at each other for some time—speechless. The man ran inside and, leaving the door open, Doug could see an antique case filled with firearms. The man fumbled threw the drawers getting ammunition and breaking the glass case. He must have been a collector of superannuated weapons. This was really the wrong person to run into.

Doug succeeded in getting up. Thank God that he could, or he might not ever have lived to see the end of civilization. Every muscle in his body helped him as if slapping him in the face to make him mindful of his predicament.

The man, who must have been Jared, had cautiously moved over to where Doug was lying. Doug had crawled over to the side window as to make sure that he wouldn't lose track of his hunter.

Just as he was peering in at him, he heard someone pull up in a black cruiser. It was Anthony's crew. They ran out of the car, and scattered individually into the woods.

They were armed with the CARPP 44 which was the second most powerful double-barrel handgun available, shooting well over thirty armor-piercing bullets a second. They had an additional weapon capable of shooting just as many soft-nosed bullets. It seemed hardly comparable to what Jared had.

There was dead silence. Then a stream of shots came from behind a pine tree located about one-hundred yards from the house that soon was accompanied by shots from another source. Doug heard Jared yell out "shit" as the whole facade of his house was being ripped to shreds. Jared, himself, bobbed down in time.

The cessation of sound assuaged the air once more. Doug could hear Anthony's atrocious laugh in the background. If viewed from a distant vantage point, the whole picture was like a scene in a play with the smoke and dust blending into the air, forming an unwavering color, resembling that of a painted backdrop. The scene had something else which made it comparable to a play. It didn't look natural: people running around in a forest like beheaded chickens, some person standing besides a window waiting for it all to pass, a house set in a perfectly plain location looking so out of place losing more of its beauty with every bullet, boisterous sounds without their counterparts—human urges to satisfy curiosity by examining what had just transpired. There was no one around to help though far away people heard.

The movement of a miniature metal cone imbedding itself into the skull of Raymond broke the silence. Jared wasn't dead. His shot brought out a clandestine monstrosity in Willy who reloaded with a new magazine and ran towards the house in defiance of the other's cries.

He ran the whole way with the trigger depressed; showering everything in sight with slugs. Consequent to reaching the stairs, his own fate awaited him. Jared jumped from behind a metal support beam and ended the torment in which his adversary lived.

It was now up to Anthony, Dirk, and Pete who presently had the upper hand even though they suffered two losses. They were also more adept than Willy, but began to get unstrung. They worried. The property which Jared owned was supposed to be his final resting place, but now it was an abattoir with the trespassers being cattle.

Confusion. No one was quite sure where to go from here. Anthony, along with the others didn't want to get away from this scene for a few reasons. One was that they weren't sure if they would make it to the cruiser in one piece. The forest provided a good shelter, but at the same time it also served as a prison. They were held captive by their malevolence.

Jared, was trapped alike. He was fearful to crawl out of a window on the other side of his house because all the windows were situated at least two-hundred feet off the ground. Plus even if he did devise a method of getting to the ground, he surmised that he was surrounded and would be eventually caught if he did try to escape. The best thing for him to do was to stay put.

Everybody didn't let their guard down even though seconds grew into minutes. Doug found the best position since he was surrounded by an old wall made of coarse sand. He managed to find an alcove between an area where two walls met. The only pitfall was that to leave this harborage he had to go through an entrance directed to the line of fire. He thought that he would let things cool off first.

He didn't have time to notice it right away since his life was on the line, but when he was alone, he saw that he couldn't prevent his hands from trembling. It was so bad that he was hitting the ground uncontrollably. Then all of a sudden he understood the jeopardy he was placing himself in. To prevent anyone from hearing the ungovernable sounds he was making with the earth he sat on his hands afraid to rest back against the wall to relieve the discomfort for fear of making a vibration. Who knew, if he had lain against the wall he might have gone right through it.

Looking though a hole no bigger than his eye Doug was able to eavesdrop, and watch the entire region around the house, acting like a genuine voyeur. It wasn't, therefore, hard to miss the looks of what was a Molotov cocktail flying towards a window on the second floor. Upon impact, the curtains caught on fire. Now Jared's duration in the house was limited. The fire was spreading slowly to the already damaged outside of the building.

Doug felt powerful, and alive. He couldn't care if the world died. He could feel the urge to survive in every cell in his body. It was strong, and nobody mattered to him at that moment. When he read about meditation he often heard about the mantra. It is a phrase that is repeated many times so that the individual becomes more focused in everyday life. Now during this anxious hour he repeated to himself his own mantra that he usually restated in a quiet room in his house, "I am powerful and alive. I could care less if the world dies."

He didn't know the full meaning of the mantra. His statement wasn't appropriate. If he had drained the vastness of ignorance that clouded his reason and replaced it with golden experience, he would have been ashamed of what he now said. A lot had to be learned.

A high pressure tank was thrown in the direction of the hoodlums, then another. Two shots from Jared ignited them. He ran out of the house following two spectacular explosions. One detonation obliterated the cruiser while the other injured both Anthony and Pete.

*   *   *

Doug couldn't think anymore about what happened. He sat in his room quietly looking out the window.

How powerful the mind was! He must have fallen asleep a few times, but during the moments when he had regained consciousness and thought about his preceding existence, he would de facto see images of his worse day alive. He temporarily erased the fruit trees he was looking at, and replaced them with images of Jared, Anthony and all the others. He could still capture the way the wall, ground, heat from the explosions, ash, and the emotions he had, felt. When he heard a noise outside he would, without knowing it, store these thoughts away and regain the view of the environment he belonged to.

He comprehended what was happening, and now brought this to his attention. He was curious about why he hadn't noticed it before. It was as much a part of daily life as waking up. When people talked or daydreamed they shut out the world, and substituted in a desired reality. Only now did he notice in depth what happened, and only now did he attempt to force his isolation from what he saw. He desperately tried to think about his best friend, Bradley. Upon gripping the abstract inspiration of looking outside a window, but instead seeing something else (almost as clearly), he right away returned to the picture of the fruit tree.

This was difficult. It presented a challenge to him. It seemed that his mind didn't want to listen to him, and he, determined to get it under control, decisively made a note to practice during meditation picturing different objects. It was hard to focus on them for as long as just ten seconds.

What he did now was different. He still pictured the objects, but he didn't fully know why. He did it to practice. That was the limit since it ensued from his second-hand knowledge from books.

He received the methods; proper posture, breathing . . . but he didn't have the enthusiasm that he now possessed. It let him ease the strictness, and be complacent with the freedom to do what he wanted. This, in return also relaxed him much more than he was. His mood gave him the freedom to control the methods he knew. With time he controlled his mood. An ever-present potential of freedom entered a portion of the mind nourished by the whole.

❖ *Chapter Nine* ❖

Trying to hit mechanical flying fish with a laser gun wasn't as easy as it may sound. Things hadn't changed much. Except of course for the laser, and the flying fish, but the reason for the gathering crowds was still the same.

Inanimate decorated sensors, that's all they were. They floated so naturally through the air not even giving the presentation of any connection to a mechanical apparatus. They could hypnotize, and exasperate you during a single shot.

Doug had hit one of them, and the lighting changed, illuminating the background with circles of color. There were so many circles that Doug got light-headed, and dizzy. The whole area behind the flying fish was filled with enough brightly colored holograms to set any stranger, walking close by, a little off balance. They resembled tiny multicolored pinwheels that used to be seen at playgrounds or virtually anywhere children used to play. How a person could concentrate with all these distractions was beyond Doug's understanding. Perhaps that was the point of it—one big distraction. It wasn't so bad really. Maybe he could get used to this. Throwing out money for the chance that he could behold the grand spectacle of a hologram. People never tired seeing them.

After hitting three of them, and missing the fourth Doug got fed up, and left, but not before he was reminded by Susi to take it lightly. They moved on to the shooting gallery. There the luck changed. A "very impressive" sign got illuminated, and Doug won a free ticket to any ride.

They looked around them, and saw nothing but desperate human beings trying very hard to be happy. They tried so hard that they recreated an altered past that brought memories which they knew could not be accurately recreated. This wasn't like the old carnivals because it lacked realness. Some said that it primarily served as a historical acknowledgment. The past, though, was lost forever, but now they were racing into the future, forming it according to a past which should have been improved upon and not poorly imitated.

In some way it did work, if the least of what it did was to get people to forget personal problems, and to reminisce about old joys. The noise from the excitement was to much to bear in some areas.

Susi said that she loved the carnival. Doug wasn't so sure he had the same feelings. He liked getting out of the house, but to love a carnival was pushing it. It came every year to the local high school by his house; a little drive into town. He went there almost every year, missing only a few visits because of work and having no one around with whom to go.

He remembered when his father had proved himself in the force test. He put everyone else to shame because he was the only one able to hit the boxing glove all the way up to a bell that gave out a "clink" upon impact. There was relatively no transformation in the attraction as time elapsed. It corresponded to the competitive nature that all people have in them. A poster by the boxing glove featured a brawny man, displaying his musculature to an audience. Just looking at this seemed to be a proclamation from the viewer: "I am willing to pay a few bucks to put my neighbor to shame." This evil part of human nature wasn't only portrayed with this poster. It emphasized everybody else's nature.

The topmost leaders in charge of the whole amusement show were strained by the community five years back to take away a ride that inflicted injuries to two young kids. Surprisingly there was some insubordination on their part. Their voiced opinions together which were found in the local newspaper: "Chief organizers refuse to dissemble ride standing one hundred percent behind its safety. Engineers stand together with them. They say that only minor modifications are necessary to restore the amusement ride to working order again without further complications."

In short, the ride was too exorbitant to build. The profits didn't start coming, and had it been dismantled, there would have been a tremendous debt. So they kept it, and covered up the fatalities by saying that the kids misused the equipment. If they had followed the instructions given at the beginning, so the families were told, then they could have precluded their injuries. It's amazing what can be said for the aspiration of maintaining an opulent lifestyle. It revolted Doug.

The two of them went on about every ride available. It was getting dark as they walked towards a frugally set up tent on the outskirts of the vast property. It was plain, and set up with the help of two trees. Over a taut string was a stretched yellow-green fabric pinned to the ground at the ends forming a triangle. It must have been used many times now because the holes near the ground were beginning to tear from the strain. A sign on top of a grassy mound before the tent said "Psychic Reveals Future." Some sumac branches covered the "Psychic" part of the sign so only when the wind blew did spectator's eyes catch the entire message.

They entered the dark enclosure. Doug turned and looked at Susi's face, of which he only saw half because of the lack of sufficient lighting. An old woman came from around the posterior side of the tent. She wore a bandanna which

Doug thought must have covered up her brittle hair for he saw a small thinning strand hanging over her right ear.

"How do you do. Would you like to catch a momentary view of the impending." She said in a somewhat cryptic tone. Doug temporarily imagined her boss or manager teaching her how to behave to intensify her mystery. He thought of her checking the bandanna in the mirror every day, and getting her look just right all the way down to the strand of hair over her ear. He was jolted with a confident understanding of her perfected but mundane job.

He pretended to be playing a game from his childhood. His friends used to pretend being someone else (taking the fanciful form of a robot, or perhaps an alien). This wasn't too different. "You may call me madam Lesley. Please pull up a chair." He accompanied the game occupied with this self-confident energy. There was a small table covered with all sorts of objects which Doug had never seen before except for the deck of dirty cards. So much scrap metal could have been easily found in a Restricted Region of the country slowly crumbling into the land from whence it came, or in an artistic studio possibly altered daily, and esteemed by an impecunious sculptor. How differently the same garbage could be viewed!

"Now, I will tell you about both of your futures. Let me hold your hands. With yours," pointing to Doug, "in my right hand, and yours," indicating Susi, "in my left." She closed her eyes, and laid her head on the children's table. The silence felt awkward. Her harsh voice pierced their ears, "You will both be married one day." Susi tried to hold her laughter in. "You will possess a home different from anything you are used to. It will be beautiful. Also you will have two children."

Trying to prove her a phony Doug interrupted and said with sarcastic grin, "Do you think so. Could you approximate this time for me so that I could be better prepared."

She raised her head and looked at both of them. "I'm sorry, that is all."

Susi didn't want to hear that, "I want to know more."

Doug looked at her shocked—shocked because he thought that she was going along with this game. Why would she want to waste any more time here? It didn't matter. Maybe, she wanted to stay late at the carnival. Maybe she was interested.

"OK, OK, but he will have to go." Focusing on Doug. "I cannot explain why, but he is distracting my energies, and I feel that I couldn't give you an accurate description of anything."

"This is ridiculous Susi. Com'on lets get out'ta here. I'm not leaving you alone with this freak show. I don't know her intentions." It was quiet.

"No, wait if it doesn't bother you I would like to stay. Let me hear what she has to say. I'm just curious really."

"OK, fine. Just be careful. I will be outside if you need me."

He walked out, and when he approached the twilight encircling the entrance of the canvas covering he heard the psychic say, "What I will say isn't pleasant, but because I fell that you believe, I think you should know. If you want you can follow your boyfriend out."

They stayed in there talking for about a quarter of an hour. Doug felt haggard waiting so he went for a walk between the masses.

He passed a poster that was hung up on what was left of an aged telephone pole. There were no wires connecting it. It was cut off halfway up, and was presumably used as a pole for advertisements. Doug looked upwards to the ever darkening sky at the poster just out of hands reach. It was a caricature of president Thompson. It depicted him as a desultory unacquainted buffoon in the framework of a cartoon character whose very ignorance turned the country into a living atrocity.

Life changed after President Fletcher's assassination. People liked president Fletcher much more than Thompson, but of course there was a slight exaggeration on the part of the comic. The president wasn't that inadequate, and even if there had been a different one, his inferior qualities, it was assumed, would have matched those that this president possessed.

The government wanted the president to fit a particular character, since it disregarded distinctiveness among role models. It controlled the way they should act as opposed to the older methods of government in which the president had a certain amount of power to do what he felt was befitting in promoting well-being in the nation. No one knew the extent of this control, but the goal was to let society run itself within some confinement.

This could produce just the right amount of chaos to rid communities of nefarious minds. The laws had changed. If a murder has been committed, the police wouldn't try hard to take the necessary precautions they once used to. They let it slip. This is how the ghettos got larger making some gang areas unbearable for living. The government knew that some people wouldn't bother to get caught up in this fighting, and they therefore protected themselves by moving to a safeguarded area. The murderers, drug dealers, and many of societies social outcasts, it was intended, would demolish themselves.

Doug was lucky to be living in such an agreeable area. This didn't mean that it should be praised without any precautions. They did have a large gate all around their estate which was incessantly watched by security cameras linked undeviatingly to the NAST security agency. This brought ease to Doug's mother the most because she often had a penchant to worry.

These changes within the organization of how people lived did have disadvantages. Many innocent people died to a lack of protection from the police. The COPS which long ago were known as the (Committee of Public Service) became familiar as a group of people removing the dead from the streets. That was all. This anger and hostility was expected from taxpayers who saw everything deteriorating. It was expected for there to be increased riots, gangs, militia groups, poverty, but the rich would likely stay rich, and getting rid of the poor simply meant staying out of their lives.

The police weren't completely passive. To those doctors, congressmen, and a multitude of people who held degrees, they demonstrated their respect with help (even if these people lived deep within Destructive Cities—as they were called).

It was one big experiment to see how things would change. No definite outcome was known, but just in case things got out of hand, the military was always prepared. Secret agents were ceaselessly roaming the streets making sure that no foreign or domestic ascendancy was plotting against their system of administration.

What resulted was still forming just as a snowman surrounded by freshly fallen snow, and a mercurial and lively child with a free afternoon. It was surprising to the government that some cities were without a scratch, and their crime rate hadn't changed much before this law. Others changed completely. The benefit was the reduction of population which was getting too high.

Then there was a turn of events emphasizing the ordinary person's inability to voice his opinions. Strictly speaking, that wasn't true. Anyone could voice his opinions, but he would have to face the repercussions resulting from them. The government completely changed. Instead of a policy of non-punishment, it moved on to a more stern approach.

There was a period of transition between this passive and the active interplay of the government, but eventually the whole society felt the changeover. The government realized that they weren't reaching their goal quickly under the old system. With some reorganization and alteration of the power, the laws gave authorities the ability to execute people much more easily. Crime rates dropped and they were still getting rid of the criminals who corrupted America.

No contrivance was completely full proof, though, as was expected. The militia groups were secretly getting stronger and plotting to rid government agencies, slowly, as warnings. They were a terrorist group that tried to halt progression. They were succeeding for some time, but remarkably once agents, which still walked the streets, found out the source of the attacks, the end was closer than anyone anticipated. Depending on the size of the undercover militia, sometimes entire armies were called in to eradicate the nuisances.

This second approach solved many problems, and kept the society safer than it has ever been. In fact, it was too safe. People were afraid to move a finger. The watchful eye would always be around them.

The aftermath of it all: the dissonance for this unbalanced living was denounced as a lack of leadership. Thompson was blamed because he was the only one whom the people knew.

The real root of man's burden was an undiscovered secret.

People wavered in their ideas because the advancement society had entered required it. It asked for a change because as the intelligence of the population increased so did their demands and strains on leadership. What people wanted was simple. They wanted order without a strong ruling hand, and yet they wanted freedom as well. It was impossible, though, to have both freedom and order. To have a structured society people had to obey laws. Obedience came from two main sources as society found out through experimentation: people would either obey the ruling hand because of their set beliefs in morality and righteousness or they would have to be forced to obey through the invocation of fear. Either framework for society required that people give up a level of autonomy for a mandate authorizing brotherhood and peace.

Almost all great cultures of the past fell because the leaders listened to the postulated necessitations for freedom; freedom for sexual pleasure, freedom to allow violence, freedom to do drugs, freedom to satisfy human urges for happiness. What is problematic is that human nature is evil. Giving in to a satisfaction of urges breaks down the rules which promote safety. Society would become a war zone where survival of the fittest becomes the new law. Strength for survival would replace organized growth. Regression would turn extension and expansion into desolation.

People needed to fight their earthly pleasures. Children had to be taught virtues that would hold them and their posterity together: virtues such as self-discipline, dependability, honesty, and reverence. Indolence would only bring violence.

Now people would have learned that they wouldn't have been unhappy without total freedom, but wholesome. They would have entered the world with goodness and dedicated their lives to helping others. That would have been where the growth came from.

This was all easy to think about. If questioned people might have even believed it and dismissed its simplicity, but the truths that it claimed could have only brought forth improvement.

Sometimes Doug thought with a childlike imagination that it would be best if society followed a path governed by beliefs established in anarcho-syndicalism. By following a doctrine by which workers seize control of the economy and government by direct means such as a general strike many injurious aspects of society could be eliminated. Industries would be owned and managed by the workers, and the powerfully domineering and rich elite that exploits the workers wouldn't be needed. It might be highly unlikely for this to occur, but the unexpected and improbable could at times present the best solution.

Doug dawdled through the carnival as empty-headed as almost everyone there. People were kept away from the genuineness of reality. Maybe only one person there really knew the truth. It was one of many possible and truthful outcomes. Relief came from knowing that free will was always at work.

During the time when Susi was with the psychic, Doug had walked around the region where the woods, and grass bordered the carnival. As he returned to the sumac his eyes were taken off the ground onto Susi standing outside the tent.

She didn't look herself. Something was wrong. He got this message when he asked her how it went. She didn't reply. Instead, she stood in place and looked ashen. He went over to her, and repeated his question hoping he would have more luck the second time around. Nothing.

"What's wrong."

Finally, she began to move indicating that she wanted to slowly walk with him. Her voice matched her pace. It was timid, and soft having a strong similitude to a stalking tiger about to display his built up aggression and hunger.

"Nothing's wrong."

The tiger stopped. He knew that if she didn't want to tell him anything there wouldn't be a chance for him to get it out of her. So he didn't pry any further. They went to see a stunt show with people jumping out of buildings pretending to shoot each other, and making much noise in the process.

After that, they went to see a display of human monstrosity. There were all types of people: from the very towering and strong to the short and fragile. Many had masks to display what once was normal. They were on the side of the main walkway gathering a crowd around them. Doug might have stopped too if Susi hadn't pulled him away. She wanted to go home.

She didn't like to see people like that. It wasn't because they were different. She wasn't repulsed or amazed by the sight of them, but instead by the assemblage of people who got a thrill out of seeing the tribulations of others. She knew that the recipients of all those gazes didn't like to be stared at or occasionally laughed at by a group of teenagers. They had to stand there and appear to like it because it was all they were allowed to do in a world filled with a classification of individuals who mixed into a crowd to look in at the elevation of their own contentment at the expense of others.

They couldn't do anything because they were a minority. Free rights to all could be shouted for eternity by the constitution, but it would never reach the ears of those few who were truly powerless. Pain was recreated from the slightly altered past that people tried to preserve.

This case was analogous to that which occurred many years ago. The numbers of native American Indians were dwindling, but that didn't mean that those that remained could be taken advantage of. Many professional sports teams took on names that were offensive such as The Redskins. No one cared. It didn't even matter because not enough voices were present to protest. It was too small an issue to worry about.

Susi was unique because her face wouldn't ever be in a crowd. Crowds generally made her fidgety so she avoided them if she could. She was one of the few people left who wasn't egotistic and sordid.

They went to Doug's house and were alone on account of his parents being out. They found a seat in the family room, and sat down exhausted after the long day. It was quiet.

Doug felt offended because he knew that Susi was hiding something from him, and he couldn't conceive any reason for her lack of conviviality. Did she feel comfortable around him?

"Did you believe anything that psychic told you?"

This came unexpectedly from her. It interrupted his train of thought, and as to get her to the point he replied the only way he knew how.

"What?"

"I mean do you think that we will, actually, get married one day?"

"I don't know." He saw her face staring at him asking him to say more, to rescue her. He spoke slowly and with restraint.

"I personally don't believe in what those people have to say. I think they are all charlatans. True psychics wouldn't be working in such places. They'd probably hide from the world or something."

"She told me horrible things. Things that would depress anybody."

"Like what?"

"You don't want to know, trust me. Let me just say that her prophesy was apocalyptic describing some futuristic cataclysm. She was vague, though, and only gave me pieces of it."

"Is that what is bothering you? I thought that I did something." Relief came to him. "Don't worry. She should be mortified of herself scaring someone for money like that."

She was a bit comforted by his statements, and rested her head on his shoulder. Trying to corroborate her unspoken belief she pressed on with the topic and inquired, "Have you ever heard of Nostradamus?"

"Sure he was a prophet born in the sixteenth century. I used to read about him."

"Really?"

"Sure." Doug said. "His father was a prosperous notary in the town of St. Rémy, Providence. His grandfather, Jean . . . ." She started giggling, and put her hand gently over his mouth.

"I didn't ask for a biography, silly. I was just wondering what do you think about his prophecies."

"He must have had some gift because he made so many close predictions."

After some time passed she added, "It's great that we have so many mutual interests. To think that I would find somebody who likes yoga, also. How did you get into that stuff?"

"Well I first started with meditation. Then . . ."

"Meditation! Wow, I also tried it."

"I hope we're not related." is what Doug said with astonishment.

"I started a few years ago. I like the idea that it helped me stay calm, and relaxed. Lately I haven't been practicing too much. I should do it more." Susi kept on describing her past experiences while Doug got up to get a notebook from his desk.

"I haven't shown this to anyone yet." He held it out to her so that she could make her judgment of it. The pages were wrinkled and were beginning to turn to a soft shade of yellow at the edges. It became evident that it dealt with his experiences with meditation as she read to herself the first two pages:

LEARNING

A droplet of water in tall grass,
reflecting colors of the spectrum,
swaying in the breeze,
barely clinging to its foundation,
waiting for it to be appreciated,
waiting for the sun to penetrate it.

Darkness.
I feel happy, then I feel nothing.
Loss, Distrust, Anger, Waste, Regret,
Anything is possible because nothing is held consequential . . .
He arrives—discretely at first,
Prying, He wants to explain all,
But calmly succumbs to silent inspiration,
Through self-discovery and cognizance,
I fearlessly understand death,
Every second it nears I feel the coming travel to infinity,
If only it could be sped up,
If only I could let another soul know,
Anything is possible because I matter . . .
Peace.

Traveling to infinity, going on never ending voyages, only to be interrupted by the sporadic false sense of reality . . .

Reality is an illusion resulting from a misguided perception. The same can be found in the macrocosm as in the microcosm since everything is in itself one with the outer limits, and creates itself by being . . .

One shouldn't undervalue the notion of simplicity. Its truths surpass any doubtful thoughts. It has a way of transcending the normal way of thinking. Without it life would be meaningless . . .

Traveling to infinity, going on never ending voyages, through endless barriers, only to be interrupted by the sporadic false sense of reality.

Susi finished reading it and looked up at Doug. His eyes looked at her questioningly. It was peculiar, but had an undiscovered beauty in it. In a flash she wanted to know more about Doug; about his life; about his fears; about his joys; about him. She put the notebook down, ever so carefully and sat on his lap.

She started kissing his cheek, and moved slowly on to his mouth.

His arms were around her. Besides excitement he also felt beatitude. This meant only one thing: he felt close to this person mentally as well as physically. Perhaps more mentally because his excitement seemed inferior. If this had been one of the snooty girls from his school he was sure that he wouldn't have the complimentary feeling he had now. He would just feel a superficial attraction. Now he was Adonis loved by the great Aphrodite.

He first took off her shirt, then her bra. He looked at the whole naked body sitting on his legs, indubitable catching the beauty of the human form in its simplicity. He felt a certain energy flowing from her as they touched each other. This fluid energy was made known to her the moment he put his hand on her navel caressing her abdomen. She sat still showing herself off for a moment, then made it apparent to him that it was her turn. As she unbuttoned his shirt she was amazed at his robust physique. He felt her breasts soothingly against his body as she pressed up against him, and they showered each other with kisses.

❖ *Chapter Ten* ❖

Doug was nice. It was a simple description of who he was. Sometimes he strayed from this character, but he always came back to it—being nice to people, animals, and other beliefs.

Altruism may be more dubious and hard to find than many think. Could altruism be achieved while a person is unwilling to overcome his corrupt nature? Some may no want to overcome it. Some couldn't live their lives without it. It is a touchy subject because it is filled with much ambiguity.

Doug had time to experience life a bit further during the next few days. He was able to expand this questionable topic. Maybe it was futile even to spend the energy thinking about it, forming synapses that didn't ever have to be brought into existence. Maybe not.

Susi was away taking a summer course. All Doug knew was that she needed help with biology. They called each other a couple of times, but because she was so far away he didn't get to see her too often.

He often spoke with his friend Bradley for hours at a time. Bradley graduated with Doug from the same school and he was very amiable, but Doug didn't like to be caught hanging around with him. Honestly, he was embarrassed of him because he lacked notoriety. He would talk to him as a friend, but Bradley was shy, and Doug would sometimes make up excuses to avoid him. It was ironic that he eluded his company because they had been best friends since they were children.

The summer droned on. It was unbearable sometimes. The sun reflecting off the tiles composing the walkway made it too painful to walk without some protection. A few times Doug ran outside barefoot only to regret it later on under his mother's care for the blisters on his feet resembled those of a burn.

Scientists said that the heat was a result of pollution. Sometimes, during the worst days, it reached 120 degrees or more outside. The flower beds were dried out, the grass was burnt, and because of the conservation law they weren't allowed to water it, should they be so asinine.

His time outside was limited since he felt most effervescent in the cooled house. To be outside, though, was to be alive for him. He walked over to the pond a little stretch away when he saw some type of merganser. It must have been starving in the little bit of water that was left in the pond. He never thought there were many fish there, but now, especially, the poor thing must have been close to death. He wondered why it hadn't gone to the man-made lake to fish. Maybe it didn't care for such a lake. Maybe it would rather die.

He saw the Northern Oriole, the Common Grackle, and the Brown-Headed Cowbird after deciding to climb a small earthen dam to see what other kinds of animals he could spot. He saw mostly birds, in truth there were many birds around his house. This was probably because there were no detriment forces working against their existence, and they had plenty of insects to feed on; for instance the Praying Mantis, the Stinkbug, the American Pelecinid, and Earwigs.

He loved birds. He admired their freedom. From the effortless gliding of a vulture to the beautiful voice of the Speckled Song Bird. They made his being complete. Every day around six o'clock in the morning there would, out of nowhere, arise a myriad of soft voices growing louder by the second as if it were their premium quality of welcoming a new and unmatched day.

Sometimes he awoke in the noiselessness right before without knowing exactly why. Then instead of startling him, the sounds would calm him to sleep again. This is how it was day after day. Even if he stayed awake for less than five minutes he still felt the urge of meeting the new day upon hearing the little voices strain as they reached their full gamut barely making it through the thickness of the house walls, and only then was he able to feel halcyon.

He drew his right forearm across his sweating forehead thinking that it will somehow help his condition. His shirt was beginning to get wet, and when he began to feel a sudden dizziness, he turned around to luxuriate inside his habitation.

On his way he walked by a puddle of water that was reduced to a circle of darkened earth with a few droplets of moisture in the very center. There he saw an earthworm very stiff, and almost dried up, but somehow still showing its last few efforts of movement. It was beaten but still it tried in vain. It was difficult for it to move because of its slowly hardening body. He stopped and looked at it struggling to survive. He thought about why he did it after he picked it up and carried it home in the palm of his sweating hand. It was ridiculous and childish, but he had nothing else to do. He poured a teaspoon of water into a small cup and set the worm into it. When it began to move back and forth violently, he knew he had saved it.

Astoundingly, he ran outside with the worm in the cup and, while his heart hammered for two organisms, he found a hand shovel and dug close to the moistened earth adjacent to the pond. He threw the earthworm in with the excess water, and left.

Walking through the torridity, he pondered why he had done it with a smirk on his face. He could have just looked at it and left without any further fuss. He could have stepped on it. It definitely would have been easier. Did it really matter? To him it did.

He was divided. Half of him wanted to be tough and meet the world with a primal aggression so that one day he could be somebody. He was able to act like this whenever he brought his attention to it. However, when he didn't think about it, his natural personality took control, displaying his nice behavior towards everyone. He thought it was because he had no self-esteem. No. It wasn't that. He was confident, but when he had a choice of helping others he did it because he really wanted to. Sometimes he felt ashamed because of his actions. Sometimes he didn't. Each separate consciousness had its moment in the spotlight about equally. He was somewhat like the people who had two personalities, except that his were more under control. They were strung together with the building blocks of equality. Each had its own job.

How could he have been like some of the barbarous honchos making it big in life (who wouldn't care about firing someone who desperately needed a job) if he felt that he had a guardianship towards everything he encountered including a measly earthworm. That was why his mother told him not to be nice. Being nice was like being flippant towards something that absolutely shouldn't have been taken with levity. Being nice induced punishment.

But what about the many religious doctrines that he read about? If consideration is shown by an individual towards another person that individual will be rewarded only if he doesn't care about the reward. This separates the greedy ones from the honest ones. He was probably doing fine in God's eyes, but how could he know what was the best thing to do. Faith turned into doubt.

In a sense he wasn't living in any world. He wasn't a hedonist, and he wasn't, what is called, a religious extremist. Since he lived in the religious, and the secular realm, he was at a loss for an identity. He was too sensitive, and caring to earn money and keep it all for himself without feeling guilty about not giving some of it away, and he was to much attached to corporeality, being brought up in a big house, that he couldn't give it up and lead an isolated life. To make a compromise such as his wasn't the answer.

Deep within his sphere, the microcosm of the world within, he knew what was the correct passage in life. From time to time he wondered if he had been born with this personality, and was highly endowed by it because he had been possibly a strong person in his previous life resisting temptation. He wasn't sure about that one, but if it was true then he was counteracting this natural tendency towards peace, trying to sustain a primitive being on earth. His meditations turned him into this mess because the peace he felt wasn't the same as the comfort derived from belittling others. He felt an elation from something that was non-materialistic. What it was, was not known to him. That was the frustrating part!

If God or some supernatural being appeared in front of him and told him what to do he would gain the confidence of abandoning his other bridling half. Even then he couldn't be sure if what he witnessed was real. He could be hallucinating. The religious dilemma was a real predicament bordering schizophrenia and lunacy.

It was a commonplace and verily prosaic thing to reflect on. The aforementioned became so ponderous for his mind to carry around that it constantly occupied his thought process. He slowly didn't give it conscious thought, and it became a part of who he was. He incubated it as second nature just like many of his instincts. Except his instincts made sense.

How could he have known now that he had to be stubborn in faith and life—stubborn in only the good aspects. When he stuck to an idea and didn't let negative suggestions corrupt his head then his mood would change according to his passions.

He was happy when his parents came home. He needed to talk with someone. The only statement he held on to the whole day was that made by his mother in the morning. "Eat the fruit I prepared for you. The grapes were expensive. They were imported." It wasn't much, but it had love hidden in its connotation.

During dinner the telecom rang.

Liz went to go answer it, and said when she came back, "I have good news. That was Rob. He hung up before I could ask him if he wanted to speak with you."

Doug's father looked on with a detached facial cast. "How is that good news?"

"Oh stop it Alan. I was worried sick about him. This is only the second time that he called since he left."

"It would be better if he hadn't called."

"Aren't you interested in what happened to him?"

Doug couldn't follow very well. He left the table to sit in his room because he could feel an argument coming on.

He loved his brother, but he lost touch with him. After all he had been gone for four years now.

He had stolen some of the family's money and ran away with his girlfriend who was six years older. Alan didn't like her, and refused to sanctify the wedding when he heard of his son's interest. That was generally why Rob ran away. Later, he couldn't get a job and due to other financial problems he had to come back. Doug knew that he ran away to a MMI (man made island) somewhere in the Caribbean. His guess was as good as anybody's concerning the exact location.

"No man is an island, entire of itself; every man is a piece of the continent, a part of the main." He was alone again. Even with people downstairs he had to stay sequestered. In an impetuous moment he remembered this line of poetry he had learned in grammar school. He always loved poetry and was muddled that he still remembered this particular one written by the British poet John Donne more than four-hundred years ago. Why had he thought of it? It was relevant to the call his mother just received in some small way, but the point of it was unknown.

In the kitchen, Alan had been carping with Liz about his son. Liz was aghast that he could forget him so quickly. He had fathered him as a baby, and now was almost willing to disown him. Her defense was stronger than his bitter memories and he lost the debate at the end.

It was the motherly instinct that didn't let her give up. She wouldn't let theft, even though it was a serious transgression, split up the family. Liz looked at One Eye and thought, "Some life. Be glad that you don't have such problems as us."

Alan remembered his own youth when he had been wild, not as much as Rob, but wild nonetheless. He felt an inquisitorial amalgam of enviousness and nostalgia. He wanted to be young again. To have the passions, and adventures that he remembered. He felt blameworthy for taking part in this imaginary evasion from a mortality he found uninviting. He couldn't envy anything his older son had or experienced so far because despite the glory associated with it there also came the pain. The pain caused by worry, anxiety, fear, and stress.

Asking to have only the positive aspects of life was not only unrealistic, but if it was possible, a person wouldn't feel any biological aging. He knew this, and he wanted to feel free again not only because of the ecstatic feelings, but because he wanted to fill his life with an ease which was unknown to the old. His disharmony with his son had to do with Alan's own fear of age.

Alan had the theory that if people rid their lives of stresses then there is no reason why they shouldn't live forever. He wanted to study biology and this curious prospect of immortality when at an impulse one day he decided to go into engineering instead. Excluding any biological clocks that may somehow be programmed into the cells, the body degenerates most probably by influences from the environment. It has the ability, though, to regenerate its injured cells at a certain rate. If the detrimental influences mar the body at a faster rate than it can repair itself, the body ages. If it fixes itself at the same rate, than the aging process is able to be stabilized and no effects of development could be seen. If, on the other hand, people regenerate faster than they get injured they could in effect reverse the aging process.

Alan's reasoning went like this. If someone could speed up aging by hurting themselves with the use of cigarettes, alcohol or other abuses, they should also be able to slow it down, stop it and possibly reverse it. Injured cells leave the body and replace themselves with fresh ones. This should go on forever or at least a very long time until the store of energy (food) is depleted. Alan should have followed his instincts in doing research. Now he was reduced to a middle-aged man living on a supply of vitamins hoping that someone else will take the initiative to continue with his past research.

Here he was. Sitting on a chair in the kitchen remembering through his son, feeling sorry for himself, trying to stay young, and unwittingly taking out his anger from desperation on his son who had his own problems.

Liz could never grasp the complex mental situation her husband was in. Not even he could understand it. He did what many people do when they are afraid of expressing their thoughts; he enveloped them with an imaginary quilt to protect his fear which had to stay inside only him.

What Rob did was wrong, no question about it, but Alan knew that he added something into his resentment, something that shouldn't ever have been there. This was aided by their bad relationship which became something that he possessed. It was a thing, and he was regretful—regretful indeed to distance such a valuable item. He was different with Doug.

Unable to cope with his character he hid his face into his hands chagrined by the human nature that he never asked to possess.

❖ *Chapter Eleven* ❖

There is a big worm chasing him. It is at his heels when he falls. Its grasp is too strong. There is no turning back. A rope made of gold is remarkable lowered to rescue him, and he clings on to his dear life that he just cannot waste; that he cannot lose. A part of him is left behind being devoured by the immense beast who is anything but helpless. Suddenly he is fed with grapes, imported ones which are very luscious. He gains dint and crushes the creature who is nothing now.

Doug woke up relieved, but with a peculiar craving, to the chime of the security camera that indicated a visitor at the front door. He was caught off guard. No one came this way. People didn't bother. He changed and walked to the door rubbing his eyes.

He saw that the man looking at him through the camera was old and doubtless shorter than himself. A short dark goatee was intentionally left to flourish, and it began to cover his lower face. He wore plain clothes made of a gray material with no buttons, and carried something like a suitcase. He was straining with a frown into the camera because the sun was just rising in the East beaming its rays playfully off of the metal casing.

"Hello, I am Will Simmons. I work with your mother. She told me that you are interested in meditation, and said that you don't have anyone around to speak to about it."

"That's right."

His voice was soft and low. It took on the form of salesman who had extensive experience dealing with people, and was so confident that he didn't have to prove himself. At the same time this voice associated with his clothes gave him a sort of spooky aura. He could have played a person possessed with by an evil spirit pretending to be nice. "I have been doing that sort of thing for quite some time now. I teach a seminar that is only a few bucks. Would you like to try it out?"

This guy needed some exorcising. Doug didn't take him seriously, but he was cautious. "I s'pose so."

He fidgeted with some papers, and uttered "great" without being completely there mentally. Alan sometimes displayed the same absentmindedness while concentrating on the news. "I got it. This it the information about where and when to go. It is pretty close to your home. You can come today if you like."

"OK, thanks."

"See you there."

He shut the door not knowing what to think about it. This person didn't seem trustworthy. Antithetically thinking, he didn't look like an experienced criminal. Also, Doug was no fledgling. He wouldn't let himself be cheated. He was his own person, and if he didn't want to pay the fee he wouldn't. He decided to go, though, and check the place out.

He communicated his intentions to his parents at work. His mother reassured him that he was a "swell" man, but to be careful anyway. He sat into his ravit which would easily get him to where he needed to go.

The directions led him to a metal shed whose purpose was ambivalent. Perhaps it was meant to be a warehouse. It gave the impression that it was just put there recently, since around it was trampled grass while if it were old this grass would have been long gone, and it could just as easily be taken away. Around the main foundation was some slothfully thrown sand.

Doug entered the superfluously lighted construction and immediately saw Will surrounded by a group of people. Each one was unique in some way. Most of their clothes weren't customary. They could have been described as people preparing for what used to be an ancient custom: Halloween. You wouldn't see these people walking the streets. Or maybe you would. Anything is possible. All that Doug thought at the time was that they were a grotesque looking tableau.

Will's eyes lighted up when he saw Doug's lone figure standing by the entrance. Doug could feel the satisfaction radiating from Will's skin.

"I am so glad that you made it. You will Not be sorry that you came."

"I hope not."

Doug paid the fee, and was told that after the procession he will hear his lecture. Procession? What procession? This was getting stranger by the minute, but Doug stayed with it, thinking that it was better in a cool shed with freaks than alone outside in the hot weather—although he had to force this conclusion to come out.

About ten people who had previously been astir began to march down an aisle which was defined only by the sickening demeanor of an old drawn-out rug getting creased as the individuals moved down the gradually inclining floor of the building. Will was already by an altar and he kneeled down in front of it. It held many fruits, and vegetables, including different sauces.

Doug had a waggish watch on the stuff. It got worse. He wanted to laugh, but imagining that he did with dreaded consequences he restrained himself. He repeated over and over biting his lip that it wasn't too bad. In this frolicsome speech of the mind he so talked to himself, silently of course. "This is exclusively unusual. Nothing else. Nothing else? The guy is worshipping a freakin orange hooded with barbecue sauce." He cracked. Unable to contain his soft laughter, he had to start coughing to follow through with a good cover-up.

After all the extravagant preliminary arrangements, the main speech began. Will was the principal speaker with the others sitting in a lotus position circuitously around him each holding a turnip. Was this guy for real? He stressed that what he and his followers had, resembled the means of enlightenment used by many religions, though he had altered them significantly. Therefore, what he had was not a religious group. It wasn't even a religion he practiced. It was a means of improving the conditions of life for anybody who was determined enough to follow his beliefs.

He called himself a Rosicrucian. He described the original and elderly meaning of this, saying that Rosicrucians were the members of an international fraternity of religious mysticism devoted to the application of esoteric religious doctrine to modern life. A lot of other personalized mumbo jumbo was added so that people understood that he was different to some extent. He finished his brief introductory speech that solely regarded events of the past with mentioning Zoroastrianism (the ancient Persian religion, founded by the prophet Zoroaster, teaching the worship of the deity Ormazd in the context of a universal struggle between the forces of light and darkness).

This ending didn't seem relevant, but the speaker looked delighted when he mentioned it.

"And so my friends, our belief is very much like that of Zoroaster. We have to understand that there is a skirmish in this world between lightness and darkness. Or better said: good and evil."

He paused to collect his thoughts for the main oratory. Doug hoped that it would be better than this introduction because he was on the verge of passing out simply from the monotony. And then Will spoke. Just as Doug had previously suspected his hidden talent, sure enough his voice had mutated. It turned into an energetic even obstreperous voice. It was as if he had this voice all his life, how confidently he used this ability. This is what he said . . .

"Guests you are here because you believe. I will let you know that you are the selected ones. You have insights. So if you let me, I will enhance them for you by discussing the sovereignty of the Self."

"What defines the Self? When a person tries to answer this he may start with the questions: 'Who am I or what am I?' These and other questions are essential in expanding a person's horizon of consciousness so that he could come to a plausible answer. Every human being has a Self, which consists of his personality, and his traits defined by heredity, or his environment. He also can tap into the Self which is different from the one just mentioned since it's a dimension separate from the body residing in God's realm, and is therefore a part of God."

"Obviously the answers to the questions just posed don't come from a few minutes of contemplation. Seriousness is the key to unlocking philosophical concepts that may otherwise be forever hidden. Belief, also a key characteristic, changes the whole person from a deluded, and unknown body to an enlightened one. Only then will the person realize that he is generally made up of a material body, and a mind. This mind is what people call the spiritual part of the being and it is much purer, and far less impressionable than the body. Being the part of the individual which is intangible, the mind has an enigmatic denotation."

"It is the dimension in which thoughts are formed. The moment a person gets a thought, instantaneously he brings it into existence. This intangible concept of the mind is able to move atoms of carbon, hydrogen, oxygen, and other particles in the brain's cells with every thought."

He paused to take a drink of some liquid which definitely was not water as Doug could see its red color from where he sat.

"Friends, this dimension of mind is puzzling and much closer to the true Self than the brain, the organ that uses thoughts to manufacture actions. The proof of this is comprehended by anybody who has ever been conscientious about doing something, and in the middle of mild concentration he receives a totally arbitrary thought relating to an extraneous event. At that moment, if the person is observant, he realizes that he has gotten a glimpse of a world of the seemingly uncontrollable, and unpredictable. The brain differs because it is a part of the body's self, which desperately relies on the other Self to survive. The body is like a sculptor, for some people it works to reveal the beautiful form underneath a blanket of materialism."

"For people in the world of today, it is difficult to get in touch with themselves, their Self. One to two centuries ago, people were more in touch with the mysterious side of life. In the present it seems that there just isn't time to do anything besides work, and when a few moments are spared, people take it for granted, saying that indolence is necessary for sanity. When questioned about the reason for continuing work they are presently involved in, they might say that it gives them the necessities for living. This response is given by those who never gave much thought to the real purpose of life."

"Is the purpose mainly to get money so that we could eat, sleep, live, and die? Those that answer yes probably believe then that happiness is the most important thing, and that living life to the fullest will eventually reach a zenith of vivacious living. To these people I can only say that they have corrupted the exultation of life. They have taken everything they could out of it, unknowingly—of course, and now left it drying up into an eventual void."

"There have been many people, some of them here with us today, who have managed to evade this fate either by luck or deep thought. They have used their ability to reason which led them to a universal logic. These people have been affected by their environment, or by reason during quiet contemplation, which brought about a crucial understanding of the Self . . ."

"For the Self to become unified with God, one has to disregard any connections one may have with the body. To exemplify this experience consider the practice of meditation. To find the Self, one has to uncover the area of the mind, that it resides in, by becoming conscious of it, and this is exactly what meditation does. It's goal is to reach a peaceful, and precocious state of mind. It involves focusing the mind on a given object for a substantial amount of time. After some time, one can feel a shift in consciousness which cannot quite be put into words. It could be considered a temporary elation of the self. Then, slowly, awareness comes back to everyday reality."

"When meditation is initially practiced, it appears to be very difficult to seize control of the mind. This is because the average or normal mind is like a wild animal which cannot be tamed without some effort. This supports the notion that the Self is at first uncontrollable, and independent of the being to some extent. It is therefore immutable.

Enlightenment comes when thoughts become slowly controllable. This happens not because the person begins to control the Self, but because he learns how to access its ever flowing energy more easily."

"After continuing the process for some time, a person changes the way he views himself, and his place in society. He will find that the Self is an unselfish and good entity which advocates peace among everything. Life won't be a miserable burden to him, or anyone who takes the time to discover their hidden glory, anymore. We could all learn that our lives are embosomed in beauty. We could learn to be delectable, and to appreciate this beauty in ourselves, and in nature. The Self is such an immaculate entity, that only a short exposure to it will continue to radiate a blithe spirit even when the subject has ceased contact with it."

"Awareness creates reality. If a person is imagining that he's sick, then he may become sick. This is seen in cases dealing with hypochondria. Also, during meditation, the shift in awareness from the surroundings (outer world) to the Self (inner world) creates an elusive atmosphere of existence. By focusing on a specific object such as a rose, man begins to lose feeling in his hands, feet, then eventually his whole body. For him, during these precious moments, the body could be assumed to be nonexistent, and he experiences a part of the Self. The only existent thing is the rose.

"When taken to a different level one can make only his Self existent, by focusing on his mind. Now, there are no boundaries which hold a human to the material world because he isn't aware of them. The same is true of the concept of time because if concentration is deep enough then no thought will exist which might question 'what time is it?' The proof is demonstrated by people, practicing meditation, who easily lose track of time.

"Only enlightenment. That is what meditation gives. This doesn't include living longer or being healthier, even though these are some desired effects which people thrive, and rely on as their sole purpose. This is a false way of thinking, resulting in a hedonistic way of living. I would like to stress that the purpose of meditation is to experience unity with everything in the form of enlightenment. This unity is a feeling of total isolation, and yet it is commensurate with an ever—knowing intelligence. These ideas are synonymous with the religion of the yogis in India. If someone would go up to them and ask why don't they visit America, they may respond, 'I am America.' Most people, though, live a life of desperation while they should lead simple lives in harmony with nature. Unity of a person with environment is a slow process, but once accomplished, it pervades everything and he coalesces with the world. God can be said to be separate from us since God is nonmaterial, but because man can be closest to God in the realm of thoughts, then he can be considered unified with Him.

"In conclusion, I say that when people strive for the fulfillment of a natural tendency in their lives (such as spiritual wisdom) then they live in a state of greatness. This is available to everyone. It's defined by the degree of curiosity someone has about life, and the amount of philosophy he thinks about. In chronological order then, unity can be achieved by doing the following: (1) being open minded, (2) asking questions which may lead to philosophical absurdities, (3) trying to decipher the absurdities created, and (4) attaining the realization of the importance of life in relation to the awareness of the perfection of the Self that brings enlightenment." He paused here finishing with a "Thank You."

A man got up from the audience, and started yelling at Will. He said that Will was a fraud, and anything but a spiritual person. Will's responded calmly. He started to tell him about the perilous doubts of a non-believer while two much bigger people dragged the man out of the shed. The little skirmish didn't change much. The audience, together, raised their voices, and it took some effort to quiet them, but the program went on.

Most of what Will said must have gone through Doug's mind at one time. He was surprised that his description of how to meditate matched the conclusions he arrived at by himself.

Following Will's speech two men took center stage and displayed supernatural feats. These were the things that Doug had read about, and now witnessed. A man with purple hair took a long narrow sword and held it in front of him with the point directed towards his stomach. He did this with a precision as if he wanted to give everyone a special lesson of how to perform hara-kiri.

He gradually pushed the sword through either trying to highlight the resistance he encountered or the great engrossment that it took. The audience gasped as the tip of the slender metal, which could have easily been called a long wire instead of a sword, revealed itself exiting from his back a distance away from the kidney area, and to the right of the spine. Sure it was amazing to see a man shishkebab himself, but only a screwball would do something like that. Doug's spell of laughter left him as he stared, like the others, open mouthed.

The man then carefully lifted his hands and cautiously moved sideways for the audience to see directly what had happened. The sooty background accented the sword's residence as it was lodged in his backside. He then attempted to pull it out, and did so with a similar ease as he had done in the reverse direction.

His troubles were greeted with the numerous spoken accolades that came from the crowd.

This was the greatest scene. The others were quite spectacular, but they couldn't match it. Who knows how many times this guy did this. He was some professional.

One person cut himself with a bowie knife, multiple times, and didn't shed any blood. Another sat underwater for a substantially long time. This went on until the collection plates were passed around, and an announcement was made about upcoming seminars.

Doug hadn't realized how late it was. It was already dark outside. Only when he did step out did he focus on his hunger. He hadn't eaten lunch.

He stopped by the door to ask how many lectures there would be total.

The people cleared away abruptly. Doug would have done the same if he hadn't gotten dizzy. It was hot inside, and combined with his hunger, and disgust from the show, he wasn't at all surprised. There were a few logs placed close by so the intention to resemble benches was noticeable. He tottered over to the closest one and plopped down.

When he came to, he noticed two elderly people sitting next to him looking and speaking with dire disappointment. The man's name was Herbert, and the woman, his wife, was Isabelle.

The presentation of their complaint reminded Doug of Bradley's grandfather. He always complained. He didn't seem to be emotionally bothered by anything, so there was no point telling him that he should watch his heart or blood pressure. He got a kick out of complaining. It wasn't because he was old. Many elderly people might complain here and there because they have needs, but grandpa Darison was different. He liked to make people jump around him, and care for him without really needing it. He said that his paltry fretting was always with him. He was the same person now as he was twenty years ago.

Doug asked them what was the problem. They said that the title given to Will by the stranger that was carried out suited him perfectly. He was a phony.

Doug defended him by saying that he spoke unequivocally about the topic with frankness even though he was surprised at this outburst since he had a reservation about him from the very beginning.

They agreed, but said that speaking truthfully doesn't alone indicate a strength of character. His actions should have backed up his preaching. They said that if he lived a life of what he taught then he wouldn't have collected money twice from his congregation.

Doug took interest in Herbert's conversation. "Listen son. I know that you are impressionable at this age, and that you must have been impressed by the display of rarity here today, but let me remind you that Will is one big walking contradiction. He forgot to mention that one has to be careful not to overindulge in the Self. Such a person may or may not achieve unity with God, but at any rate, he should help others come to the same realization that he did. It is essential that the society also evolves spiritually. Indeed there is a delicate division between seclusion and society. People shouldn't revel in any one too much. The best is a balance."

"The people that showed remarkable things are the bad ones. They are using their power flamboyantly. They should be bettering mankind without being showy about what they can do."

"And as for happiness, environment has little to do with it. People find this strange, but its true. There are people who have had hard lives and live in poverty, but they may be happy. Others could have had everything but be miserable. It takes an effort to be happy, and those who try will find that they can influence themselves. The effort brings on the mood and joy. Joy doesn't come by itself. If people don't try they can never achieve peace."

It was hard to say how old Herbert was. His looked to be sixty, but once he spoke to Doug, his voice had energy. It wasn't horse at all. Contrariwise, it was temperate and soothing. This dissolved any first impressions one had about his age. Once he spoke, it was virtually impossible not to be anchored to his youthful tongue while deducing his age. He was unique. He was anachronistic.

Herbert knew a lot about spirituality. He was a vicar and spent much time meditating. That was why he came to see what he could learn here. He told Doug his experience, and said that he would be willing to teach him if he wanted. They became good friends after that meeting.

Doug learned from him that life was filled with mendacity, and that to avoid it one would have to be aware and slick. Doug's life was the past and it was so vital in influencing the future. If some small change could be made hundreds of years ago by going back in time, the person responsible would come to a present very different from the one he had left behind. If Doug hadn't met Herbert he could have turned into a different person.

Fate, then, was as fictitious as Will's voice. Destiny didn't exist. People had to make their own lives up from scratch like a carpenter building a house, and just like a carpenter, depending on the person's incentive he may be pleased with the elbow grease he put into it, distinguishing between a beautiful house, or one that barely stands, falling apart first from a poor inside support, and then making its disfigurement known to the world from the outside. The success a person has with his free will depends on judgment and determination.

❖ *Chapter Twelve* ❖

The message said that they will be late. A delay, extra work . . . there could have been numerous reasons for it. In any case, this was exactly the break that someone needed to render further worries to Doug's family.

The noises emitted from the nightfall during this late hour were exceptionally strong. Insects seemed to be shrieking, inducing discomfort into the air instead of succoring the nerves of an overworked person to fall, blandly, into a relaxing sleep. Outside, it became a jungle-like abode of survival, instead of a paradise. It became wicked; almost frightening. It made you want to stay indoors to avoid the dampness, ticks, mosquitoes, and environment in general which sent out a premonition of misgiving. To add to the burdens of the night was the complete darkness which didn't allow any starlit walks, any heavenly admiration, or any interaction whatsoever. The moon was an absentee from this particular night, afraid of its own lack of courage to unveil itself.

A distant barking of a dog, gave the idea that an infinite amount of rabid animals were roaming the land concealed by the blackness. If some unfortunate individual did walk outside protected by a personal maker of light, it appeared that the surrounding oblivion, proving itself stronger, would swallow up any trifling attempts made by this flashlight to even get the familiar reflection often seen in the eyes of a neighborhood cat as two headlight shine into them.

He had a great time. He felt happy, but this air around him impacted with the negativity of the climate. It was enough to change his mood.

Doug had just taken Susi home. They had dinner together, and enjoyed every second of it.

He got out of the cruiser, and tripped because of the darkness. It was his own fault. He parked far from the motion detectors on purpose so that his parents didn't know that he came so late. He walked into the house using the back entrance.

He thought that his patience would prove valuable. He didn't know that it could, actually, steer him into the wrong direction. Once inside he turned the door handle so slowly that he heard the ticking of the alarm an uncountable number of times. Each tick was about a second apart. As he moved the door closer and closer to the wall, he put his finger on the front edge so that his finger would be the first to touch the door frame. This prevented him from poorly estimating the distance he had left so that he wouldn't slam the doorway shut. Then he locked up the house without making as much as a vibration.

He acquired this marked skill of entrance since his first intimacy with Susi. No one ever really knew when he got home. Sometimes he arrived at four in the morning. Other times he came earlier. It didn't trouble anybody. His parents trusted him. They didn't have any reason not to. He wanted to spare himself the trouble of answering the exasperating questions he would have to face in the morning.

Thinking they would be asleep, he tiptoed into his room. A flashing crimson light caught his eye before he reached it. It meant there was a message. He thought that it could have been Bradley. Oftentimes he left messages without any real purpose in mind. He was still a kid at heart, so Doug wondered if he should even bother checking.

It seemed strange that his parents hadn't already looked, though. He turned around, and walked over to the machine with the same careful precision as before. He checked it. The message said they would be late. His parents must have been working overtime again.

He did this all for nothing? He yelled out loudly, and turned on the lights. How much better it felt to welcome himself into his house! He went into the room One Eye slept in and fed him before he jumped into bed.

It was always a relief to put the day's events aside and think of nothing. Nothing was wrong with him before lying down, but he felt better once he did. At intervals in the past he couldn't sleep so easily as now, and this was because he was continuously trying to figure out some problem that was drilling away at his mind. He wouldn't rest till he fixed it. Be it a computer error, a dilemma in school or even at home—he would stay up in bed thinking about it, and not making much headway.

He soon had enough of it all, and it took a higher understanding of his life to filter his priorities out of the ever-growing mass of information he put into his head daily. He realized sleep was more important. He used methods of meditation to tell each part of himself that he will focus on these problems another time. He believed that the body worked as a whole under the influences of the mind only when it was at peace with its separate parts. In other circumstances of uneasiness and strain, the body was rent asunder from its unity. That's why when people face troubling aliments, their overall mood must be brought into play so that it could aid the isolated obstacle. Then the body fights as a whole. Depressed people let the individual areas of their body fight alone. Hence they aren't as effective in curing themselves.

He finished his self-help session by imaging the world around him being covered up by a giant blanket. Any problems that occurred, took on the forms of sharp defined beams of light trying to pass through the protective fabric. If the glimmer of light increased, he increased the layer of aegis. Only by distancing himself was he able to find an entente between his many regions.

A ghostly rumbling sound came front the downstairs. At first, it was faint, but later it grew louder, reaching maximum intensity at short intervals. Doug was startled. He lost his concentration. The blanket disintegrated under the light beams that savagely destroyed its very fabric. It couldn't maintain its existence for very long. In a flash; a fireball, it was gone.

Doug scampered to the machete that hung on the wall on top of his mirror, overlapping it. It was a gift Bradley had brought back with him from Puerto Rico. He knew that Doug collected knives, and thought that he would love it. Doug loved it, but he never showed such a level of kindness or generosity in return.

Now seeing its worth, he empathized with his friend who tolerated his delinquent attitude well. He felt thankful, and yearned to express this thanks to him. He grabbed it, and crept along the wall towards the location from which the sound streamed. This wasn't enough, though. What if the person had some better weapons? He stopped, went into his parents bedroom, and opened the safe to get the particle gun his father owned. He walked down the stairs.

He had many questions. How did this intruder get passed the alarm? Did he hear Doug yell to himself? It boggled the mind. In the dark, he saw a lone figure throwing things into the air near his fathers work place. There was a small light shining on the operation.

Doug had to do it now. He turned on the main lights, and hid behind the stairwell a substantial distance aside. The person turned around. It was Rob, drunk as a sea captain! He let his dark beard fill the blank areas Doug used to see on his face. He had one earring, and a necklace both made out of what looked like garbage. His girlfriend was an artist, and she sculpted these things for him so that he could always be with her in spirit. She wore jewelry that was a duplicate of this. He rubbed his eyes, and yelled in Doug's direction.

"Who's thar?"

Doug remained quiet.

"Who's thar?!"

Doug put his weapons down, and stood up. "Rob? What are you doing here?"

"Nothin'. I just came to check."

"Check what?"

"Nothin'."

It was clear that Rob wouldn't give him any answers. Doug walked up to him. The mighty stench of cognac on his breath hampered his resolved closeness. Doug just stood looking at him. Which is more than Rob could do. He barley kept his eyes open. He just looked unabashedly at the floor with his eyelids halfway shut bearing a close likeness either to a really arrogant person or to the living dead.

It was during the observation of his condition that Doug saw the floor covered with some papers. There weren't that many pages littering the ground because all the information in the house was stored on software. The few legal documents which Alan had were kept in folders.

"God, what were you doing! Why were you looking through dad's folders."

"The man . . . ." Rob pointed behind him towards some area in space where a man should be standing just as he lost his balance and fell.

Doug was determined to get it out of him. He shook the older and stronger, but demoralized version of himself hard.

Rob spoke while stuttering, "OK, stop. This man, h h . . . he approaches me. Tells me to check some files. So I d do it." To emphasize his words he poked Doug in the breastbone with his finger.

"Who?"

He was out cold. There it was. The implacable situation Doug faced. He could never change what he heard or what happened. He could alter it, and see if his parents buy it, but he was convinced that on his deathbed he would see the representation of his inebriated sibling directing his attention to the floor like a doltish harlequin playing dumb.

❖ *Chapter Thirteen* ❖

The explosion was big, and unexpected.

He could have had training in the military, or in the boy scouts. Maybe he was just one of the deranged people who plan for every possible crisis. The group of people who ruin their lives planning for something that might never happen. They range from those who fear intruders to those who fear life threatening diseases. Jared belonged with them and on the day of the attack he wasn't helpless. He was ready.

Pete, and Anthony fell backwards from the blowout. It was hard to tell how badly they were hurt from the pergola-like enclosure where Doug hid. Dirk was the only one who was left unscathed, and he intended to keep it that way. He ran behind a paving stone waiting for the others to finish the calculated job for him.

The fire from the molotov cocktail was spreading quickly because the wind started to pick up. Quiet fell upon the scene once more, except this time it was broken by the crashing of the roof. One would think that it struck the second floor in the middle where it was weakest, almost intentionally, so that it could reach a more comforting resting point on the first floor of the house. It turned the house into a giant letter; that of a "V." The desolation to the house paralleled that which could have been committed by a tornado, having an irregular and unpredictable path of destruction, headed towards a dreary house somewhere on tornado ally in the southern United States. The fringes of the house stood untouched, but gave no support to the center that caved in like a giant rotting piece of wood.

Jared was still inside, somewhere. A person demonstrating an ability to confront trespassers and manslayers wouldn't let the collapse of a house stop him. He would win the battle or die fighting. His father was the same. He resembled the men that people read about; finding tremendous willpower in a moment of urgency, and above all never giving up. When the officials found that man in the desert a while ago so dehydrated that he couldn't even bleed from the lacerations he had until he was given enough water, no one would have been surprised in the town of Ellenburg if that specific news glorified Jared's father as the survivor.

Someone who can beat all odds and amaze doctors in the course of events has something inside him whispering the values of life in his ear despite the environmental influences facing him. Is it a subconscious act? Can someone be born with such a will to live? If it is not in the genes, then it certainly must be from the environment. Though no one is sure, it must be a little bit of both. People who triumph over cancer, survive great ordeals, or live to be one-hundred and twenty years old most probably live every second of their lives examining an objective that they never take out of view. It is a part of a personality. But a personality can be altered.

Jared learned it from his father, his father from a harsh life always having to fend for himself. Since he wasn't given everything at birth, he didn't grow up facing the world nonchalantly. He fought with an eagerness that was supported by every emotion of sanguineness he had forced into his veins.

That was why four people were having such a hard time dealing with Jared. Everyone thought otherwise, though, when his contour was beheld by Dirk for only a jiffy which was long enough for him to permeate it through the window by opening fire. Jared yelled, and a series of thumps were heard as he fell down a flight of stairs.

Doug gave a trembling sigh of relief and somehow thought that it was concluded.

From the confusion he had experienced, he thought that Jared really had been the bad guy. He didn't even think about the bomb anymore since his thoughts were preoccupied now with much more dramatic thoughts. He entered a state of shock that sprang from the panic in his stomach and the heat, which was becoming unbearable near his feet from the ablaze house. It made him think irrationally. He would soon be fried. If any more wood fell, it might land even closer to him. He had to get out of there.

He crawled out, and into the house through a hole in the wall. It was like being in the depths of the Netherworld: flames all around him, smoke taking its time to rise, sparks and flaming coals falling from above. He would definitely have choked from the smoke had it not been for the many oxygenated ventilation craters in the roof of the dying house. The flickers of sunlight shining through the black poisonous haze were rays of hope.

His preposterousness led him to yell to the others. "It's over. You got him." He thought that he would be under the protective hand of Anthony. He was wrong.

He should have known that only he was the guarantor of his future well-being. Up till now he was exercising his circumspection over himself very well. Perchance faltering was inescapable, but he made the same mistake as so many legendary hero's of action-adventure movies did. A soldier who just got the hell beat out of him is left alone with gun in hand, a psycho-killer tied up by a scared family with loose string—these cases are made up to increase suspense for entertainment, but it could happen in real life situations. On the screen it looks tiresome to see a man of distinguished valor make such a mistake. Only when confronted with a real life or death situation will a person realize that fear really makes one act capriciously.

Relief makes one lose the natural sense of danger. Doug had the upper hand, by escaping death, and was free to run away, but because of his clouded perception he became careless. He made a move that endangered him. It was like playing a game of chess. One couldn't back away and waste valuable moves after planning a strategy of either attack or resistance.

Shots were directed in his direction. The echoes deferred their use of the air as a medium for travel for the occasional compression and rarefaction of a sound generated by a yelling person.

"It's me, Doug!"

"I know."

"What?!"

"Doug?"

This last voice clearly belonged to Anthony. He seemed surprised that Doug was alive. He wasn't the one shooting, though. It was Dirk that was enjoying this fiasco. Doug recognized that it was Dirk's mischievous vociferation by the "I know."

A bullet hole produced in the side of the door right next to his face about one meter away is how close he came to losing his life. He still yelled above the gunshots when he lay on the ground with his hands held on his head as if a cop were frisking him. A red coal was burning his leg, but it didn't bother him. It wasn't bad compared to what he got himself into. He would get a blister, and maybe a third degree burn. He accepted it.

Doug ran to the case filled with weapons. He put an automatic pistol, and a revolver into each of his side pockets. He slung a bolt-action rifle across his shoulder. With his free hands he grabbed a breechblock rifle and a shotgun. Now the antique case was empty. A sliding drawer revealed some ammunition that could easily have been too aged to work. Lastly, he took the bullet proof vest off Raymond, who lay at his feet. He could feel the palpitation of his heart as he raced with an imaginary enemy to put it on first.

The best place to be was out of that house, so Doug broke through a window opposite his previous hiding place. He hid behind a rock, protected by dense shrubbery.

By this time Dirk was impatient. He emptied at least three magazines into the house which would account for at least six hundred individual shots. They had enough to ward off an army. Something can be said about a society which has the ability to offer this type of weaponry to youths. Their intentions for the night, involving Jared, didn't require it at all, but because of Dirk's presence the group was forced to take it. In order to understand why he wanted it, one had to look at his past.

Dirk wanted to join the Army Reserve. His father was in favor of the idea. In fact, his father taught him much about survival. This training was different from that taught to Jared by his father because with Dirk it involved a dependence on weapons. When Dirk was young they hunted deer together. When he was a child he always carried a knife in his pocket. His knife collection grew with the years until he was legally allowed to possess fire arms, then he gave it up. Of course he would have preferred the newer weapons, but that was only for police and army use. Soon he obtained black market weapons, and went everywhere with them.

It was a common sight to see a police officer on his porch speaking to his mother. They put him in jail. They confiscated his weapons. He went to juvenile detention centers. He got his license suspended. Nothing stopped the sustenance that supplied his life of embezzlements and offenses. No jail could hold the adolescent long enough. To stop him, assuredly, one had to alter his mentality, and since that was close to impossible, the police should have dealt with him, when he came of age, with the same mentality that judges retained while convicting serial killers: thought of execution.

A society shouldn't have to provide for an individual which goes against its progress. That individual could be replaced with someone much more advantageous: someone willing to help the whole, and focus on the betterment of himself and others.

Consequently then, Dirk overdid it on the day of the attempted murder. He took more guns than he would ever need. If he were stopped by a COP, then the same merry-go-round of his life would yet again take one more familiar turn. He would be out of jail in less than two years.

He acted like this for two reasons. A part of him was showing off in front of his friends, and another part, the one influenced by his father's instilled lessons, found a security in invoking fear in others.

There was a long-winded period of wait. Doug could have pretended to be dead, but it was likely that a search for his body soon would have been underway. They were going to ride it out; to see who had the greater nerve. Doug knew that time was one thing that Dirk didn't have. His impatience would soon leave him. Sure enough, soon Dirk stepped out into the open area, wearing a black vest.

Now was his chance. Doug could get him, but he was still a little far. Dirk inched forward with his CARPP 44. Doug aimed.

In view, out of view, in view, out of view . . . it wasn't any good; his hands trembled too much. He was apprehensive as his foe got closer. He hoped—"Bang"—and missed.

More gunfire, more noise disturbing the already too disturbed environment. Dirk ran. He didn't think that it was worth it to stay now. He was there an unduly long time, and now he was putting himself in jeopardy. Silence for the last time.

*   *   *

It was over when he started blathering to himself. He should have known that it was over, but he needed an extra sign. He couldn't just leave. That wouldn't be moral. His dubious spirituality told him that it would go against things in which he almost believed. Displaying Cheyne-Stokes Respiration was satisfactory for him. It meant the end. The teamster, gangster, and even communist, Anthony, was dead, and Doug slightly regretted that he ever went over to the spot where the two bodies lay. He should have left with Dirk.

He did feel some commiseration for the dead. He wasn't heartless, but upon some consideration of the matter he thought of himself as a pinko who was in sympathy with the communist doctrine.

It wasn't important what happened. It was behind him. He couldn't change things now, so he tried not to think anymore about the lifeless bodies of Pete, and Anthony.

He shivered, this time from the cold, while huddled in a natural corner of a forest formed by two large, recently fallen Boxelders. The ground was marshy, and he wouldn't have sat down if he hadn't really needed the rest.

The beauty of the full moon was overlooked. It was superficial in relation to the needs of survival. It looked unreal, and things viewed with a perfunctory observation couldn't be important. Momentous influences on the mind, however, got priority for the expenditure of energy biding the fulfillment of a desire. The frigidity spreading through his feet was real. It was felt, and its foreign presence screamed to him for attention.

A philistine dreaming of material cloths, and some comestibles—bread, corn, chicken, beef, a lobster, some fine cuisine—this is how Doug lived for eight days. He wouldn't pay attention to anything else. Moss was his pillow, and hunger his guide. He didn't have Jared's training in the means of clinging to life, but he did match, if not surpass, his determination.

He couldn't call his parents. What would he say? "Hi this is Doug. I saw a few people die today. Could you pick me up?" That wouldn't work. They would be shocked.

He overestimated their anger, though. They would have rushed to help him if they had known his position. They would have talked about what had happened afterwards. After all he didn't do anything. He didn't even know of the plan his enemies had. He didn't look at it with this point of view. His mind was soddened with pusillanimity, and his fear took over telling him that he could ride it out by himself. Again he didn't think rationally which was a major setback. He was afraid to do anything. If he thought more clearly he might have been able to come up a plan to get home quicker, but the way things were he was happy if he could feed himself, and put off the thinking for another time.

He didn't even want to hitchhike or call a cab because he was afraid that that would be evidence against him. If caught and interrogated, the cabdriver could even have testified. He could have describe the condition he found Doug in: bloody, and ripped cloths, wild and desperate eyes, hair made up like a plebeian, and it wouldn't have helped him. He didn't risk it.

No human contact, and moving as far away as possible from the place of slaughter were going to be his priorities. Despite his precautions, the authorities could have traced his friendship with Anthony, and asked him a few questions when he had gotten home. They could have put him in prison in all likelihood for life, and so he would have had to think about an alibi before he saw his parents.

He decided to walk back home, and come up with a good excuse about his extended period of travel. He thought that he could make the trip if he rested frequently. To him it wouldn't have taken long because he remembered how quickly the cruiser got there. Of course, he wouldn't be traveling over ninety miles per hour, guided by a satellite.

The first night was rough in the wetlands. In the middle of the night his shivers woke him up, and he decided to crawl into a log partially hollowed out by the aid of Father Time. There he rested till morning until his hunger woke him up. He looked around at the scenery, and took off.

He crossed a field of purple wild flowers that were abloom. They were all the same and dominated the landscape rapaciously, preventing any other species to grow in that location. He walked on for about three miles until the dense vegetation forced him to continue on the highway. He walked on the shoulder looking at the ground.

When he used to hike long distances with Bradley, he found that by looking at the ground he didn't get so fatigued. He could walk miles without realizing it. Bradley said that this was so because it was like thinking of the present. No worries were in mind, and you observed the ground as you walked almost always surprised at how far you went when you finally looked up. When you are concerned too much with looking back, then you may be too confident about what you have accomplished. It resembles a person who lives in the past, and therefore making no future for himself. A contradistinction to this is when people look far ahead of them when they walk. A person doing this doesn't achieve much in terms of progress. It's like always thinking about the future, and being anxious about its outcome without working in the present. With Bradley, at one time, Doug conquered a part of the Appalachian Trail. They hiked for about four days then, camping when they got drained.

They weren't much, but these thoughts helped him. He got caught up looking at the ground, occasionally bringing his head up so as not to run into a tree, and thought about his life. His daydreaming took his mind away from the imbroglio he was in. Before he knew it, he found his way to a small food store. Next door was an even smaller hunter's store with fishing equipment, cloths, and sports equipment.

He didn't want to use any form of payment that had his identification on it, and since he didn't have cash, he decided to swipe some commodities. He first went into the hunting store, and stole a compass (until now he didn't know if he was going in the right direction). With the compass, all he needed now was knowledge of survival.

In the other store, he made sure that no one saw his face as he walked in. He grabbed some pumpernickel, cookies, and a carton of milk and walked over to the exit. There he stood while the manager walked by him. He waited till he was the farthest he could be from him, and ran. "Hey" was the only thing he heard from the man. He ran fast. He ran far. He got dizzy. Never had he thought that he would steal anything. Crawling into a rusty sewer pipeline that was never placed underground he caught his breath, and ate the evidence.

This is how it continued for seven days. He relied on his perspicacious knowledge of nature that told him which berries to eat and which ones were deadly. He also ate mushrooms. Only the ones with pores were good. He remembered that. The worst that could happen with a pored one is that he gets an upset stomach, but if he ate a disagreeable gilled one, he would have died. His primogenitors came from Europe. His father told him about some of the traditions and customs the people had there. He checked the family history and learned about mushrooms. Upon hearing that an experienced mushroom gatherer could find them very delectable, he began to educate himself. One night he tried some with his father. They both were absolutely sure of the specimen's edibility. They survived. Even under Liz's strong dissension.

Despite the wisdom which he carried, he still didn't fit into this environment, and he didn't like it. Before he was always in control of his life, and got whatever he needed from his parents if he could show that it was necessary. Now things were different. He was still in control, but without a directing hand. He was tourist lost in a large city hoping for someone to stop and direct him. He stood out distinguishing his difference like a house plant cooped up all winter in the dark, and then set outside with unusually large leaves unadjusted to the burning sun.

It takes the human body some time to adjust to its environment. With time he could have lived more primitively and could have lost the weak leaves replacing them with smaller adapted ones. The harsh environment would have seemed milder soon. Then, if the environment was hotter than what he was used to, for example, his metabolism would have become efficient. He would have sweat less, and the strain wouldn't have been felt as much. He grabbed on to this idea and caressed it, not having anything else in which to believe, and wished it wasn't fiction. He needed help, and if no one would have given him any, he would have had to find it inside himself.

On the eighth day he felt he was close to home, yet he didn't recognize any landmarks. He walked by some houses next to the road which his mother would have characterized as being "sad." She came up with this expression once when they were on vacation. It didn't mean that the houses were disgraceful, or ugly. These houses were quite to the contrary. They were inordinate; beautiful, but their location was very bad. "How could someone spend so much money on a house, only to smell the exhaust fumes of cars all day?" she used to say. She preferred a small house in the countryside.

He walked until he reached the bordering line of civilization. The line was very distinct. Workers had been cutting away at the forest for fuel, and the bare land with only stumps looked peculiar when it clashed with the greenness of the woodland of which he now was a part. It was like a common scene from the rain forest, except this one was found in the vicinity of America's highways. Remarkably, some of the world's rainforest survived industrialization because of the many environmental coteries situated in the United States. Now the danger was coming home, and the same actions were needed. He walked onto the sterile land with discretion. There was no way of hiding here if he was confronted by someone.

He fiddled with the small wooden crucifix in his pocket which was handed down to him by his father, and which he always carried for luck. It was smaller than the palm of a child's hand, but detail took over at size's expense. His grandfather made it out of hard cherry wood. The two gracefully patterned pieces of wood were held together with a single reddish-brown nail eroded away over time with traces of iron oxide on its surface. It was remarkable that anyone could have so much patience in carving something that small. Doug thought that it regularly helped him in life, and he didn't ever want to part with it because along with its beauty came a sense of solace.

In his other pocket lay the automatic pistol, obediently waiting for orders. He didn't risk taking the other toys with him. They rested at the bottom of a large lake close to Jared's home. He had to be somewhat careful, though. The cruiser was in pieces which forced Dirk to also travel on foot. If they met, Doug wanted to be ready. He wouldn't throw away the upper hand he had in the chess game of his being.

When his fingers stopped inspecting the ornamental pattern on the cruciform symbol he was able to redirect his attention to others things. He looked at the stumps which he began to see more and more of. The stumps were waspish objects in eyes adjusted to comeliness. The same was true of the logs apathetically thrown on a pile still with some withered leaves connected to their corpus, besides a barbed-wire fence dragging out into the horizon. And some horizon it was! Nothing like that which might be seen by the captain of a ship who travels on the Danube river: a reddish sky perfectly coalescing into the clear sapphire or murky waters. It was much different. The workers on this development looked out of their houses at night to see a horizon of industrial pollutants, chemical mists, and the befuddlement of nature in all its ignominy mixing in with a childless landscape. There was no glory here. No human could find anything appealing about those transgressed logs, except the man who bought a new estate by reason of their incineration in some electrical plant considered to be efficient.

He was some distance away from the forest when his sleepy eyes focused on the barbed wire fence contained by the front of a plane that would have otherwise given way for his passage. It must have enclosed a segment of the worker's area to prevent theft. He saw the fence in front of him at the last minute because dusk was approaching. It appeared to have been transfigured out of the shadows behind it; not really existing before Doug made it out.

He didn't want to backtrack his progress so he heartily decided to scale it. Once inside the compound he would have to scale it again to continue his homecoming journey. He took off the bullet proof vest, and snared it on the barbed wire. As he jumped onto the other side, he heard a long ripping sound as his pants got torn all the way up to his thigh. This was the finishing touch he needed to actualize his ruffian-like image.

Doug looked up, he looked up, Doug looked down, he kept his gaze steady, Doug kept his cool, the stranger likewise not having a reason not to. This is what Doug encountered once inside the compound: his past fear began to exhibit signs of life as he saw a man's frame, far away from himself, walk in the direct path of travel as he was, except in the opposite direction. Here he couldn't hide. Could he turn back? How? Jump over the fence again? No. It would arose suspicion in the person. As the situation stood, the person probably thought that the approaching individual was one of his fellow workers because he raised his hand in greeting. Doug dithered as he replied with the same greeting.

He couldn't pass this person. That was crystal-clear. It was too late to turn back, so the only option he had was to turn either left or right at the corner of a building, once he got the chance. Presently, he had two elongated brick buildings on both sides, restricting any course of motion sideways.

The man, whom Doug observed to have a hat on, got awfully close now. Close enough, probably, for him to notice Doug's ripped pants. Doug shunned him during his next few steps, and, therefore, was luckily able to sidestep him.

He left his vest on the fence, and couldn't return for it now. He somehow had to spend the night here, and look for it before dawn. He had no idea where he was, and he didn't want to run into that man again.

He came upon a warehouse similar to that outside of which he met Herbert, and Isabelle. The doors were wide open. It was an invitation he couldn't refuse. There was a pile of wood chips on the side which made a great natural mattress with the wooden beams holding it in place, the bedstead. They were the finest one's there, and the pile was high enough to almost touch the warehouse ceiling.

"grrrrrrrrrrrrrrrrrrrrrrrrrr . . . rrrrrrrrrr." A faint noise was turning daintily on and off. Was it a running machine? Wood chips falling into some crusher? His senses must have been deceiving him, but he sat up and prudently listened to make sure. It could have been the blood pounding in his head alone, giving him the migraine that he never before suffered from.

A shadow moved on the floor. He was able to make out a dark spot the size of an Afghan Hound which had been softly growing. It obviously was just as much, if not more scared than Doug. This hound belonged to one of the employees, and wasn't put there to take on the duties of a watchdog.

Doug murmured quietly to it, careful that his words were inaudible to anyone who might be outside the storehouse. The insecurity of the dog gave him confidence. The canine stopped, and looked at him. Doug crawled down the pile at a leisurely pace to the spot where the dog stood. He moved so slowly that by the time he got to the bottom of the chips the dog sat down. Before this happened, though, the dog gave out one random burst of energy. It directed itself away from the boy by springing backwards. This was more out of a fear than out of anger. It was caused by a fear that called out to the beast to keep up its guard at just the right moment when it was beginning to get hypnotized. After the fear passed, the trust came back. The boys warm and gentle eyes spoke of repose.

Doug had the "patience of a squirrel" inside. He often used this phrase because he knew what self-possession they had. As a youngster he observed the squirrels on his property as they stole fruits of the many fruit trees his father had possessed.

A child with a homemade slingshot in his hand sitting on a moldy stump could learn a lot by watching nature. During summer vacations, he would sit for hours watching a squirrel gawk at him. Sometimes to pass the time, he read a book. It was a struggle between the two. It wanted food. He wanted a development of persistence.

Once he caught one of the critters in a trap he built himself. It made a lot of noise, and jumped all over the place. He carried it into his garage, and sat down looking at it thinking, "Your not so tough in there." It stayed just as still as if it was on a tree, ready to make a leap for freedom given the chance. Later he released it, and saw how it scampered away with felicity.

He caught them in this manner until one day he found one dead in the cage. "Oh God, I didn't want this to happen . . . No." Those were the words he repeated over and over silently. He killed it, and for no reason whatsoever. It wasn't quite his fault, but if he hadn't set the trap it wouldn't have happened. He felt guilty, and went in to cry.

His brother comforted him, "Hey, listen it probably had a faulty heat valve or somethin' ya know. It might have gotten a heart attack. Think about yourself this way. You probably helped the species because you eliminated the week ones. What if this one had some young with the same condition. Five squirrels, all with faulty heart valves. You saved them the suffering they would have gad during a similar death. Commend yourself."

He didn't buy it. He had to live with it. Sure it wasn't too serious a crime, but he remembered, and it would stay with him till his own death. Now he suddenly respected them, and in his life he learned that the instincts of many animals are sometimes better than his ego driven ones. It took a death to acquire the virtue of patience in life.

He had much more inner strength than this dog, and could sit there all night if he had to. When he finally got to him he put out his hand and gladly received the licks with which the dog covered him.

At last he climbed to the top of the pile again. There was a giant fan near the top of the shed that was at eye level with him. It kept the workers, who cut lumber, cool in the hot summer days. Someone forgot to shut it off, and it was slowly running. He could see the moonlight clasp the tops of some of the outside trees in the distance from where he came. An occasional falconoid bird searched for prey below. It circled with such certitude, that it reminded Doug of a hungry vulture scavenging for dead animals.

Doug was happy with himself. He evaded getting killed and getting caught by the police. He thought in his moment of rest that he knew everything. He felt independent and powerful.

He didn't know everything, though. The rationale for Doug's contentment, his act of decriminalization procured by his scrambling away from the recent past, was based on and clashed with his inability to grasp the intricacy of the superficial existence he was a part of, relevant only to the onlooker . . . and ironically he failed to grasp this abstraction even while in a room where the presence of a spiraling fan revealed the moonlit reality outside only when it wanted to as if it were emitting stroboscopic lighting on an altered reality, making sure that anyone looking through it into the night was nonplused.

PART 2

THE SECOND GENESIS

❖ *Chapter Fourteen* ❖

He looked outside his triple glass window protected from the abstruse world. Was it better to see nothing than to see water? There were only a few glimmering lights enveloped by the darkness, but those that he saw provided little comfort. They looked too small to believe that life could ever exist in their vicinity. Recalling the events of his life building up to the posterity of which he didn't want to be a part of, didn't help resolve his dubious future. Doug wondered if it had all been somehow intended; if all the sacrifices that were made gave room for some outer development. He couldn't think of what was still to come so he spent his energy on remembering the elapsed days of his disconsolate life . . .

*   *   *

He woke up, and saw a mackerel at level with his own head. It swam around in a small circle only to get back to the same position it sustained before as if it hadn't even moved. It did this repeatedly, and it was the only trick that it knew. In different receptacles, also built into the wall, there were fish resembling cod, and herring.

The bigger reservoirs were much more breath-taking, but he had to share these with everyone else, and he had to walk about half a mile to get to them. They contained Shortfin Mako, Spotted Seatrout, Yellow Jack, Tiger Grouper, Warsaw Grouper, Gag, Albacore, White Marlin, and many more. Despite their variance, most of these fish had one thing in common: they were gamefishes of the Tropical Atlantic, and they seemed to get as much divertissement by being the center of attention as the people got from perceiving them. Now and then they would gracefully swim up to the glass, and linger there for observers passing by to see. Therewith, at feeding time, they would linger a bit more emphasizing their great learned ability of procrastination, and display of certain authority, while getting to the food.

They didn't need the food. It was something unnecessary because they were always well taken care of. As in many cases, a need doesn't become obvious until every contained desire becomes unleashed while chasing down its tempestuous fulfillment.

Their manifest jubilation forced a person passing by to recurrently conjecture to himself, "Who is the prisoner here? Am I looking in at captive creatures, or are they looking in at me from their fairyland where they have everything and more than they could ever need? People always like to see on the other side of the fence. They want to know how it feels, and as the cliché goes, the grass always looks greener on the other side. A businessman could come home tired and look at his dog, and say "I wish that I had your life. All you do is eat, and sleep." He envies his companion because his point of view tells him it *must* be better. If the man relaxes and rids himself of the disposition which gave him such a faulty perspective, then, with a little conviction he would relish his actuality. Someone may fancy the life of the fish without understanding, undoubtedly, they would have been happier in the wild, finding their own food, surrounded by a harmonious freedom whose playful melody is in unison with the independence of their actions.

Doug liked watching them, but he realized their confinement was a burden to them and to himself and, upon perceiving that, he lost all interest in his observations. This burden was less a result of an indirect perpetuation of their confinement by his previously tireless gaze than a loss of the delicate balance between the interconnected framework governing the emotions arising from innocence and guilt; two sensations or impressions which, though different, are comparable, like lightness and darkness. This personal equipoise of his fashioned from a deeper totality of balance favored an unharbored and disliked guilt, and so, annoyed, he looked around his new room instead.

The wallpaper on the wall was plain, but everything else looked ethereal. This was because the color of the water from the fish tanks reflected upon everything in the room. Where there should have been white light, now existed an artificial blue.

It was difficult sleeping here. There was always some dread present—something speaking of doom, auguring a breakdown of the weak infrastructure, and surrounding foundations. This wasn't likely to happen, but for people prone to worry, it was a feasible reality.

Liz, therefore, wasn't devotedly attached to the idea of designating it a haven. For her, the surrounding water from the fish tanks resembled the vast ocean, and her living quarters a brig on a ship without any particular destination.

She didn't have any choice of her own to decide whether or not to stay. It was not up to her. It was not even up to Alan. The stay was a necessity protecting everybody, and not just any single person. He couldn't threaten the people he loved by making a regrettable decision. He grabbed the only option he had which was good enough for him. He didn't complain, but he wasn't happy. He merely existed.

They were the fish. They were in a situation where they had everything. It wasn't necessary though, and it was an immense price to pay for the freedom they lost. They missed making choices such as just going out and driving around in the countryside. It became a life of concealment, and solitude, nowhere to turn, and no way to escape. They were told that it just takes some time to get used to it, but they knew that it was more than that as they listened to the continuously present melody whose dying playfulness indicated the eventual demise of their independence of decision-making.

As for Doug, he missed One-Eye. The friend who saw him through everything. He was always there, and became like a person to him. He missed much about his character: everything from his daily welcome, to the expression on his face—his eye specifically. That eye he looked into stabbed him through the heart when he sometimes carelessly threw One-Eye's dinner on a slightly defiled plastic dish. The eye seemed to convey the dog's complete feelings; "I am better than this. You can't treat me like an animal because you know that I have transcended that title." Whether it was devotion or audacity, the outcome repeated itself every time he made the error: One-Eye would turn around pretending to lose his appetite until Doug convinced himself that he made a social blunder, and served the food on a cleaner canister. In this manner he kept reiterating his love for him.

He had gotten used to him so much that even after escorting him to his new home, and proving to himself with tears of sorrow that his departure was for the best, there were moments when he wanted to call out to him, believing that he was under the bed or in a closet somewhere. When he realized that he wasn't, his body united with a forlorn feeling caused by the tipping of his mental balance not so much under the weight of an old faux pas, but under that of his present guilt.

He activated the luminous lighting, took his grandfather's cross off a stool, and got up. It was cold inside, just like the environment on the other side of his bedroom wall. He was very indolent these last few days. There was no urge to do anything, and he felt like a rancid piece of butter that was left outside, intended to go to waste. He could have used the exercise facility, if he found enough strength to get up, and initiate the first move, but he disregarded this idea after seeing the task presently facing him.

He took out a small knife, and walked around the crumpled, and degenerated brown boxes with his personal belongings that still needed opening. He happened to open the box containing his hobbies first.

He sat on a chair, scratched up on purpose so that it looked old—on this one it just looked like a waste of work, and looked through his stamp, and coin collections that he garnered for years now. It was difficult to find stamps nowadays since they were discontinued, but his parents knew a few people that could help him, and this is how he made his aggregation grow. His mother really started the hobby when she was a girl. She cut, and sewed up plastic sheets with a piece of paper between them so that the stamps could be well preserved, and appreciated. She continued like this until she filled an entire album.

Some of the most beautiful stamps were those created right before the Broad Cancellation. They had many elaborate, and ornate background designs, and the large number, $1.10 (the ending price required to mail a letter in the United States), was always ingeniously commingled into this background. He inspected them for some time with an eighty year old magnifying glass that was taken from his antique collection.

The coin collection interested him a lot more. He found a coin from nineteen-thirty eight which said Deutsches Reich on it. Could that coin tell some history! He lay back looking at it without the aid of the light. He just wanted to hold it and think about how many people hated it, held it, wanted it, or fought for it. He thought about whether anyone died with it in their pocket. He could only make presuppositions about what it went through, but how he loved doing it.

He put it back into its holder, and then placed the whole binder on a nearby shelf. When he had finished unloading his belongings he pulled out a small box from the bottom of the crate. He knew what it was, and he was angry that the people handling the packages did such a lousy job. They could have damaged something in their neglect.

He opened the two boxes which he placed his book in before he left. The corner of the outermost box was crushed in, but the second scrawnier one was intact. He opened this one to look at what he prized most: a small ebony book which wasn't in the best of conditions. Its cover swung loosely with threads dangling a few inches below the reader's hand, resembling cobwebs. Doug wouldn't dare cut these off. Every part of this text was going to remain in the same form as he when got it.

One day he found it in his brother's room. Rob said that he could have it. He couldn't care less if he had it or not since he couldn't understand anything anyway.

The date on the first page, following a transparent piece of white paper, read eighteen forty-five. The cover was made of leather, and it had four decorative circular beads made out of bone, two made out of glass, all spaced out to look appealing. There was a small brass lock that swung around so that when someone was done reading it, it could be secured shut. It was a masterpiece.

Whether the brass lock was shut or not did not make any difference to Doug. The contents were secured, and out of his reach because they were written in an antediluvian language whose modern counterpart was equally outlandish to him (the whole thing was written in an old form of the Czech language).

If he could travel a few generations back in time, he would find his roots in the Czech Republic.

He wasn't as lucky as his brother, Rob, who got a chance to visit the republic. He stayed back at home with a baby-sitter because his parents thought that a funeral was no place for a three-year-old. Today his distance from the mother country didn't seem important until he rediscovered this book in his collection.

He wanted to know what the book's contents were about so strongly that he opened a Czech to English dictionary, and started looking up individual words. It didn't help. He could have been there forever, and still not get anywhere because the letters looked differently than those used today. He only considered their meaning, with his speculative attitude whose origin was set in the academicism he was given at birth. He immediately decided to ask his parents about it when they got back, and he couldn't understand why he lacked interest in it before.

He had time to kill, so he started pronouncing some words the best that he could. The more recondite they sounded the more he urged to decipher their intangible denotation. He stumbled through the first paragraph:

> *O pane Jezisi, Kriste! Pastyri dobry, zachovejz spravedlivych, obrat hrisniku, budiz milostiv chudym, souzenym, nemocnym, nuznym, umirajicim, zemrelym. Smiluj se nademnou bidnym hrisnikem.*

This passage was especially intriguing for him. It comprised of concepts that were out of his control. It became something forbidden even. He alone could have never mastered this book, and it made him irate but it enticed him at the same time. The basics of Latin that he learned in school, allowed him to assimilate it with this language.

Since he already knew that he had done just about as much activity this day, as the fish that were looking at him, he decided to go all the way. He lay down, and thought about whether he would ever get the chance to travel abroad. He didn't do too much pondering for, consequent to closing his eyes, he fell into a deep sleep like a tranquilized person not caring if the sun was out or not.

*   *   *

Rob, Liz, and Alan had arrived. It took three hours out of their lives, but the memories of a dying heritage would stay with them, and would compensate for their loss.

Rob hadn't envisioned the Czech republic to look like this. The modernization was there, but it just hadn't matched that which existed in New York State. The contrasts from the United States were great, and he strutted around with an air of importance when a customs officer confirmed his citizenship.

After the funeral of a distant relative whom Rob saw only one other time in his life, they stopped in Prague. There, the differences became even more distinct. It was an old city, yet to be pervaded by technology. From its beauty it seemed to be doing fine without it. It didn't need great bodies of knowledge because it had something more special, which gave people, as much if not more, satisfaction. Doug strutted no more.

Prague was an old lady who tried to hide her wrinkles. No matter what she used to cover them up, there would always be a slight indication of what she really looked like underneath her masquerade. Many of the old statues had been eaten away by acid rain. Next to them stood a picture revealing the astonishing original forms the artists meant to express. Several times sculptors mended some of the more important buildings and statues in an attempt to preserve their youth. They never were the same as the original pictures. Some were left alone. Rob couldn't see how anyone could have said which ones were more beautiful or worthy of this change since they were all majestic.

He wished he could have lived there. Rob's premise that formed the basis of this conclusion to stay in that exotic land or, at least have an extended stay, was that that place was like the combined sound of an organ and chorus whose euphonious sounds lured him to it, almost mesmerizing him. They visited Hradcany Castle, St. Vitus' Cathedral, St. Wenceslas' Chapel, and the Charles Square. Each site they saw was going to make it more difficult for his parents to pull him away from it. During this sightseeing, they also had the opportunity to taste some Bohemian cuisine.

They couldn't stay long, though—not just because the hotels were expensive, but because they made plans to stay with some of their other relatives in the remote town of Picin.

Picin was even worse than Prague—much worse. Maybe time stayed still there. Maybe the people didn't want it to move on in the natural order of things. The town was so small that if enough of these people didn't care about the outside world, then they had the power to keep things the way they were. All that Rob could say was that it was peculiar; like something out of a museum. In some areas, it didn't even have a paved road. This didn't matter because even though it didn't have the beauty of the statues, a few miles away, to back it up it had its own unique pulchritude.

Pine forests were of the only type to be seen. The tall slender pines made the ground look malleable under the dead needles which were the forest's turf. While ridding along in their rented car Rob saw meadows between clusters of these woods which were even more beautiful than those at home. He estimated that the grass, and flowers came up to his waist, and the blossoms together made the pasture-like plains look as if they were all of one color: ruby red.

They finally stopped at a wooded gate. When they killed the engine, they became a part of this area. Now they were not only spectators, they were filled with everything around them: the air, flies, woods, flowers, local dogs, cats, mice, rats, unpaved roads, and all the quaint houses. It was all inside them, and they felt it. It was a good change.

Liz didn't find these houses "sad." No, she was seeing correctly. She saw the holes in some stranger's roof, old bicycles rusting outside, old unpainted walls waiting for a small breeze to blow them over so they could die. In spite of these things she thought the houses mirthfully stood under the heavens containing their owners.

They rang a bronze bell that was attached to a small shredded string. An old lady opened the gate. She was dressed in a muumuu covered with small bright posies. Everyone hugged her. Rob didn't know why since he didn't know her, but he went along with it. She was such a distant relative that Rob told himself that she was just a family friend.

Liz spoke, "Robby, this is Manya. I know that you will really like her once you get to know her." Then Liz stopped and looked embarrassed. She didn't want to be rude by talking in English. She humbly ceded her feelings to Manya the best way that she knew how. It looked like Manya understood by grabbing the sides of her clothes as if she was going to kirtze and making a disgusted face showing that she would have dressed better had she expected their coming.

They walked passed the chicken coop whose gate was so crooked that two of the chickens were in the yard which slowly was becoming a new coop. On the way to the house Manya excitedly took the broom made out of a galore of thin birch branches which had become smooth, nearly polished, in view of its immoderate usage on the chipped tiles they walked on. Liz had to console her so that she wouldn't make a fuss.

Was this the future? How could it have been, when people used brooms that they had made themselves? Years ago people may have cloistered into disbelief had they been told that nothing would change. The prospective future they awaited was somehow different.

That was just an image, though. No one could have predicted with certainty what he was to encounter. When it arrived the future surprised everyone, just as it should have. It was composed of many different images; some virtuous, some technologically astounding, some depraved, and some, though few, had elements from each category or brought their own elements into play like Picin.

Inside was a man who didn't fit into this house just as much as they didn't. He was in fashionable attire except for the hat that made the rest of his clothes look comical. It was practically an antique; something that people wore in the nineteen fifties. He might have worn it to look facetious, or conceivably just to keep the flies away. Be that as it may, he didn't know, or didn't care. It was just a part of who he was.

He must have also been a visitor because he was waiting for Manya to come back. He sat on the seat cushions of the wooden chairs near the kitchen table as if they were dirty and he had to avoid any prolonged contact with them. He sat on the very edge, leaning back to give the sense that he was comfortable, and rested his forearm on the back of the chair without touching it with his hand. He got up to shake their hands.

His English was very choppy, but he spoke as if he had easily mastered it within a few months, using the pauses to emphasize the point he made instead of putting him on the spot.

"Hello, my name Seth. Howdoyoudo?"

Alan answered, "Well the ride was a little too long for me, but I guess that I can't complain." He was interrupted, and told by the guest of the house that he should feel free to wash his hands. He added, "Where are you from?"

At this, Seth sat back down.

"I live herr in Prague, but sometime I travel to US . . . for business. I am friend of Manya, and thought I help."

"Help with what?"

"Her friends come today to celebratt daughter's wedding."

Alan, and Liz felt awful. They planned their visit at the worst possible time. They thought that coming one day earlier wouldn't hurt anyone. Alan told the man to tell Manya he's sorry that he imposed his stay, and that he will help her prepare for her guests' arrival.

Manya's feelings were understood through the badly spoken English relayed to Alan, and through her actions: she wanted them to stay and enjoy themselves.

After Manya mollycoddled Rob to her satisfaction, she took everyone through the house. Of the whole tour, Rob loved the attic the most. The part of it closest to the stable was filled with hay. He knocked himself down as if he had carried the mass of an anchor with him the entire day. His feelings turned on him. He felt disgruntled, and bored. Manya left him alone when she saw that he wanted to sleep up there.

Lying on the hay, he opened his eyes, and saw the animals below him. The half of the attic he was in ended abruptly. There was no railing to protect anyone who might have been searching for something in the night without a light source from plummeting to a viable death.

Rob saw piles of chopped wood, and wood to be cut. In a different storage area, he saw lots of coal. Beside it stood many canisters about his size.

With child-like curiosity he wanted to scrutinize his new territory. He saw a few boxes piled right below him. A few large nails whose purpose once must have been to support some shelves were imbedded in thin boards that consisted of the side wall. He climbed down using them as he would a ladder. He reached the bottom, just as he intended, but not under the conditions he wanted. Touching the last nail, which had been bent upward but now rotated in the opposite direction upon the slightest sensation of pressure, his foot slipped and he tumbled ungainly down into the boxes for whose existence he was grateful.

Luckily nothing happened. Had he fallen from a greater height, he might not have been able to extricate himself. But as things stood, he got up as if nothing had happened, picking off pieces of hay.

In a dark corner of the stable he saw the stuffed head of a male deer with magnificent antlers. It was ruined. The skin, treated with chemicals, around its nose was peeling off showing a grotesque piece of moldy black wood underneath. It was something a nightmare wouldn't hesitate to possess. Because of the dampness, it probably couldn't have been mounted inside the house. That was why it was thrown away. Rob jumped back when he saw the two glass eyes watching his every move without blinking.

He rushed to get out of there, but first he put the boxes back only after he looked through their contents. Next to some pictures, he found old world war two pins which soldiers used to wear on their uniforms. What he did next he never intended. It just came to him, and he, not being strong enough to resist, accepted it. Then he loved it. He grasped the pins, he felt powerful and alive, he put them into his pockets—for him the world died.

He saw a small book with a brass lock. It looked very old, but the dust on it told him that it wasn't touched for a long time. He perused its contents, but he didn't get anything from them. This wouldn't fit into his pocket, so he held on to it, more interested by its uniqueness than by its history.

That was what their trip was like. Doug only missed out on meeting some relatives. All in all it was better for him with the baby-sitter. Manya let Rob keep the book after she saw his deep interest in it. Alan, and Liz helped with the party, and were able to enjoy the company of many new people. Rob unearthed his first feelings of rebelliousness that would have under different conditions stayed dormant in the dark regions of the stable.

*   *   *

Alan was miserable. Ever since he changed his job, and everything else about himself, he couldn't look at the ignominious image that challenged him, daily, as he went into a bathroom to clean his face. It was just a mirror. It shouldn't bother him, but it did, and it wasn't the mirror that was the problem. He could get that same feeling from any shiny surface because it would always show the same thing: a weak person forced away along with his family from a beautiful life.

When they first arrived at the deep sea laboratory, Doug liked it. It had fish tanks on display (there were even a few in his room). The accommodations were more than adequate, and people were very cultivated.

What was wrong? The sun would be a nice touch, perhaps the sound of a summer storm generating devastation some distance away, or even better any live animal or insect which wasn't forced to live in a cage just so he could observe it.

The underwater facility was huge. Fifty percent of it was just the laboratory. NAST had many projects underway there. There was a mineral division (of which Alan was part), an engineering division, and a new energy division. These were the only one's of which Doug knew. There were many more.

The whole facility was made of a new age plastic material that was clear as Plexiglas, yet not as brittle. This served as the main structure, and it was about six feet thick all the way around.

In some areas an outside diver couldn't easily look in because of the cement foundation. Inside the dome, it was like being on dry land. People built buildings, and if they wanted a window, they just didn't fill in any mortar.

This was how Doug got a first hand view into the depths of the Pacific Ocean. The windows looked like the skylights of a house, but instead of being built in on a roof these were on the walls. Also, they were surrounded by so much plaster that they were like little tunnels. Doug could easily have crawled into one, if he had been captivated enough by the wild ocean, to look through the dark water. He didn't though. The idea never even crossed his stream of thoughts.

So they were all living in a deep sea laboratory. It was different, unusual, and necessary all at once. Their neighbors were the families of scientists, mechanics, and bureaucrats who were forced to tag along because of a lack of job opportunities on land.

Liz also worked there. She changed from the high paid position she used to hold to a secretary-like person. If Doug had wanted he could have walked to her in about fifteen minutes, but he didn't want to be a disturbance. Rob worked close to her in a low paid clerical position.

The Tunnel Rail was out of his grasp, and so everywhere he went he had to walk. Their dome (HYTRE675F) was connected by a short passageway to another one (HYTRE676F), and so on. There were a total of fourteen domes in the HYI8764653 TERRITORY. Some of the neighboring territories had even more.

Liz, Alan, and Rob looked at their habitat as a modification of their normal life. A great modification! Doug surpassed that image. He knew it was a modification. This left room for him to form a reaction to this assessment. As always his direct and kindly response to things was based on what made him feel precious. Making him feel anything but precious, this place's repugnance had to face Doug's powerful, and alive being, which became stronger every second from the personal mantra which he now repeated, "I am powerful, and alive. I couldn't care if the world dies."

❖ *Chapter Fifteen* ❖

"When are you going to arrive there," asked Liz?

"Soon I hope. Don't worry. I'll tell you when I get there." He looked at the time. "You know I hate going to these things, but it's part of my job."

He walked out the door into what he imagined would be a routine atmosphere. He did it many times (too many times), and regretted leaving his family behind, but realized that if he didn't, he wouldn't be able to provide for them anymore.

Business trips weren't necessary anymore. People could speak with anybody they wanted to, at any time. That companies still called people together on some occasions was solely for the purpose of socializing. There was a small fear that because of vast communication networks, people would forget how to deal with each other in person.

Maybe that already happened to Alan because he found it personally engaging, and comical when he looked at old executives, who dressed up in fancy clothes, sitting around a table to bewailing over the frivolous aspects of life right before starting a meaningful discussion. They complained, for example, about the food they ate, how hectic their trip over was, or maybe even how difficult it was to sit for two straight hours during a flight—everything. It was petty talk, and they seemed to enjoy it because they had to. They were just trying to avoid what researchers said was a growing trend of lacking human contact. To him they were all careless clowns.

He received a call last week which stressed an urgent meeting to be held at the Cascade MMI. He hated going to those places even more than ordinary business trips on land because he felt uncomfortable living in the middle of nowhere. The trips always brought out a subdued instinct of fear which nature supplied man with long ago. It got weaker as people became more civilized, but, sometimes, it still managed to stick its head out from under the layers of refinement.

At odd moments, Alan wondered what would happen if all the computers on the Earth just stopped. He would be stuck on some Man Made Island until people could get back their immemorial skills of shipbuilding so that they could come and rescue him. Along with this, there would also be a temporary hunger pang among the population because all of the farm equipment was run mechanically. Many farms didn't have more than five people maintaining it.

People would be tamed and abused house pets who weren't cared for anymore and would be left in the wild to die. They wouldn't need to be tied to a tree with a leash, because they would be sure to find a way into death's hands by themselves without the aid of a malicious being. The difference between pets, and people is the owner. Pets aren't smart enough to lead their masters, but people are. When viewed in a different light, though, there is one similarity: both are dependent on Him, whether He resembles mankind or technology.

There might be some recovery from an absence of computers, but that should be left to the philosophy majors to ponder. The main problems would still pester everybody, though, and the chaos and dismay created would be endless.

So one could ask whether there is any point to rationally contemplate that outcome. It seems that only when problems occur do they merit anxiety. Otherwise a person could easily become demented. That is when Alan tried to stop thinking. It was better to be sane without worry.

He arrived on time, and spoke with Liz just as he said he would. Next, he rented a cruiser. He had a map, and directions, but it was still difficult for him to find the building he was supposed to be at in one hour. He stopped a few times asking for Henrieta street until he found it.

Off of Henrieta was a relatively small one-way road leading to a five-story building. This building stood out from the other structures because it was the tallest there. Usually, his business trips were to cities, and he found it strange that this time a few trees, and local homes surrounded him. More strange to him was that the closest city, named Honiara, (in memory of the capitol of the Solomon Islands on the northwest coast of the Guadalcanal since its devastation during the war) which was also the only one on the island, was ten miles away. The meetings were always in some city because of the easy access to vast information networks. The farther one got, the less were his chances of truly being open to the world.

Despite his doubts of getting to the correct address, he finally parked the cruiser on the side of the road, and got out to stretch. There were no numbers on the building which he assumed to be because of the construction. A plastic material covered the front of the building. There weren't any workers to be seen, but by the condition of the facade it looked as if they were putting small decorative tiles all around the sides.

This building looked quite new. It didn't look more than three years old. The houses around it, however, which dwelled between many dead trees, showing the governments lack of deftness with afforestation, must have been between ten and twenty years old. The oldest of which had paint peeling on the sides, shingles falling off the roof, and had a poor excuse for protection with a rotten picket fence surrounding the entire holding.

The advantage of not having to go into the city was that the air was cleaner here. A light breeze constantly blew, reminding Alan of the short vacations he used to take to the beach.

He wanted to ask some of the locals whether this address matched the one clearly seen on his papers, but giving it a second thought, he decided just to go inside. He opened the door, and saw a couple of companies' names on a big "welcome" board in front of him. This was the right place.

He followed the instructions which took him downstairs to a door labeled: "The NAST Subdivision–meeting today."

Inside there was some art on the wall—all characterized by the use of distorted figures, and exorbitant color. He guessed that they all fit under fauvism.

In front of the artwork, he found a dainty old polished table with individual executive chairs all specially placed, making it look like they agglomerated the whole setup into one big mass. There didn't seem to be any division between where the table ended and the chairs began (at least not from where Alan stood).

Where was everybody? He was somewhat early. Maybe no one arrived yet.

There was a closed door to his left. He sat down, no less than five minutes, to wait, when his friends, Randall and Sanford came out.

"Hey guys where is everybody? I'm not late am I?"

They responded in an extremely saccharine tone, "Oh no. We were just in the other room getting ready for the presentation on energy. Would you care to join us?"

Even though he knew both of these people, they were still comedians to him. He expected them to act diplomatically in a formal occasion, but this was pushing it. Alan wanted to burst out laughing.

They spoke as if they constantly mocked the world around them. They were like the executive clowns. He knew that Sanford, one of his closest chums, couldn't help the way he acted. In truth, many people couldn't. They were born looking at their character and seeing it as a norm. Even Alan subconsciously sometimes treated others crudely, but he wished that he could meet more people that truly spoke what was on their mind sincerely. Those people were a dying breed, excluded from society by natural selection. It was better to be disingenuous, to lack in candor. It was a way of life, and only family or good friends excepted the truth—others got offended.

Sanford was an older man with gray, and somewhat curly hair who walked shakily and slowly as if he had all the time in the world to spare. He knew Alan for eight years now, and they became good friends. He wore reading glasses, and refused to wear a watch. Alan knew why. In the past, he struggled with heart trouble, and his doctor told him that it was because of his up tight life. Since then he refused to wear a watch. He relied on his friends to tell him when important affairs took place, and felt happier knowing that deep inside he didn't really care anymore.

Randall was a very different character, almost Sanford's opposite. He was shorter than Sanford, and he rushed around a lot. When he smiled his gums looked swollen and infected as if he had pyorrhea.

Alan didn't really know him very well. A few infrequent and ephemeral hellos in the hallways at work were the limit of their mutual esteem. They still held each other to be friends, though.

In the other conference room, which was even more beautiful than the one he waited in, he encountered four more people: Marlene, Caitlin, Vincente, and the ever disliked Andrew. They were all seated.

Randall went over to a virtual screen, and began to prepare some notes. With his back turned to his supposed audience, he said, "Ladies and gentlemen, we have a lot to accomplish today. That is why we will have to stringently start as soon as the others get here."

They mostly waited in silence, each preoccupied with something, except for the few succinct conversations which the women initiated.

Finally, Randall spoke again, though this time in a softer tone to Andrew. Everyone was able to hear him anyway.

"We can't wait any longer for Luke to show up. Do you want to start without him?"

Andrew spoke with an air around him that gave everyone the message that they should treat him as a pundit. Alan couldn't stand him. If he could go back and change his life, he would have chosen a new profession, not because he disliked his work, but because of this one man. Hearing the question, the head clown put on his mask, and looked awkwardly pleased, and agitated as he spoke.

"Sure. If he's late, it's his fault. He'll have to somehow catch up later."

After this was said, Sanford absconded briskly out of the room, excusing himself for some urgent matter.

In a microsecond, the tone changed. The room looked different. It became shocking; filled with baseness. Andrew didn't look humorous anymore with a particle gun in hand, pointing straight at Alan. The action was beyond words.

At first, Alan thought that it was some kind of gag. The seriousness of the act, though, made him feel so uncomfortable that he felt his blood rush down, and away from his head. He felt faint, and he must have looked very pale.

One of the women in the room, Marlene, shrieked. Randall vaulted up out of his seat with great ease, and impounded her cries behind the respect he instantly made her build up for him by shoving her into the lighting system. She stayed on the ground covered with glass and a few cuts, afraid to even breath.

"What the hell are you doing!"

"Something that I wish I could have done long ago."

"What?!" Alan was in disbelief. The impact and deviation of the interruption from the normal course of events, which he expected the meeting to encompass, was so gigantic that the moment it happened, he couldn't believe it was real. Alan doubted his very existence. This was like the unreal situation that his son faced a while back. It was either that scenario or it was so real that every neuron in his brain focused on what was happening. The concentration was like that experienced when some horrible accident happens, and the individual is able to witness it all in slow motion knowing that a possible disaster can occur at the climax. It was so intense that he felt as if he was having some out of body experience. It must have been unreal.

Andrew spoke slowly, and with a partial grin, "Now, I want to ask you a few questions. You are friends with Luke. Is that right?"

"Yes."

"Good, I'm glad that we are on the same level. What did he tell you about the energy projects associated with NAST?"

"Nothing."

"Come now. We have been following him for a long time." He paused and laughed to himself while he looked at the ceiling, carefully pondering what he will say. "Your life means nothing to me, but if you help me, we will both forget this ever happened." He took a grape off the table, and threw it into his mouth.

"Who were the other people to whom he said that he spoke?"

"I don't know. I told you. He didn't say anything to me. If there is something, he didn't want to involve me in it."

Andrew guffawed, and showed his solemnity. There were two small explosions followed up with some smoke that clouded up the room. That was all that he needed, two shots. His comical mask hit the ground. Two lives were gone, and in front of Alan's eyes. He turned on the ventilation to clear the smoke.

Randall ran up to the two bodies whose existence ended practically before they were able to register any fright. He on the other hand did, and foresaw it in advance, muttering to himself in the direction of Alan, "You coward . . . ."

Everything was done remarkably quiet. The only loud sound was the shriek which must have shaken Andrew.

"It's a shame. Marlene, and Caitlin were good workers. See what you did. This wouldn't have happened if you had been more careful about what you said. As for Randall, to give it to you straightforwardly, I never in effect knew the man."

Alan got up with rage as he gripped the table with one hand making a clenched fist with the other.

Vincente walked over to protect Andrew, saying, "I wouldn't do that if I were you." He waited, and then begun to shout when Alan didn't budge: "Man use your common sense! You don't have a goddamn chance."

Alan sat back down, hopeless. He felt so powerless that he just gave up. He kept the strength in him asking for a fight locked up as a last resort effort of self preservation. Now he wanted to appear weak, as if he didn't care what happened to him. Only with this attitude, might his antagonists put down their guard, believing that they won. Then all he would have to do is use every beastly, and pitiless force available to make a run for it. No matter how savage an act he would have to commit, anything was better than dying. It was risky, but he didn't have any other choices.

Unfortunately what went through his mind didn't reveal itself to the others. Sanford came back from the room with the distorted art paintings. Alan shouted.

"Get out! They just murdered two people!"

Sanford could have easily let him know that he was acting stupidly, instead he just said, "I know. Trust me I don't like it, just as much as you don't, but it has to be done."

Alan's desperation came back. This time it was no act. There was silence.

"Oh God. Why did you have to be a part of this?"

In the middle of his explanation he saw his friend's body. "Well you see I didn't really have much of a choice . . . he paused when he saw Randall . . . you shot Randall?!" He turned to Andrew. "I told you not to hurt him."

"He was causing problems for us. He was just in the way."

"No. No. It shouldn't have been like this."

He ran, crying, to his comrade who was still alive. "I'm sorry."

Vincente became annoyed. "Damn it don't back out on us now. We have a job to do. Lets follow up with the procedure."

He grabbed Alan under the armpits, and threw him into a storage room Andrew just opened. He wanted Sanford to do all the work for him. "Talk to him will ya. I don't think that I can get anywhere. I'll be outside watching the door."

Sanford languidly got up, gently putting Randall down as if he were a newly made piece of delicately hand crafted crystal. He whispered a few words into his ear which Alan couldn't hear.

Andrew was inside the room taking care of the bodies, and cleaning up the mess. Sanford walked, as if he were drunk, over to where Alan still lay. "What did Luke tell you?"

He didn't answer.

"Anything? Come on. He must have said something. We are sure of it."

Andrew came back and slipped into his ferocious personality again. "Let me handle it Sanford. You have to be tougher don't you see? You take care of the place. Make it look like new." He sat down on his left leg and rested his arm on the knee of the other. "I'll show you something that will make you talk, or at least get some kind of reaction from you."

He opened the only door left in the room, out of which Luke's body fell.

Alan was even more dumbfounded, and he entered a state of shock, not even being able to cry. He wasn't angry anymore, just repelled. He felt sorry. Sorry for Luke, and in some loose connection he was sorry for Andrew, that he became such an epitome of iniquity.

"This is like from some great movie isn't it?" Andrew paused just to look at what he thought was one of his inferiors. He thought swiftly around. "We know that you were one of Luke's confidants. He entrusted you with information that was to remain untold. What else can I say? You have something we want, and we have your life. You don't even have to say all that he told you. Just tell me how many other people he referred to, or how many he intended on talking to. When you are ready I will listen, and then let you go."

"How do I know that you will keep your promise?"

"You don't."

❖ *Chapter Sixteen* ❖

Memory. It is everything, and it is nothing. We live knowing how to walk, talk, eat, and sleep. Some of this lore is a moiety of a collective memory handed down from previous generations which gives us instincts, the rest is that which we build up ourselves. The memory from our undergoing with the environment.

Of what is memory made? Could it be that the messenger proteins, CREB and BDNF, give people the ability to live, or does human memory come from a different connection? The messenger proteins could only be a medium for receiving information from some higher source. Even if one is able to uncover the secrets of this higher source, it would still be a perplexing life because the predicament of finding *its* creator would remain. Human thought doesn't have the ability to understand the essence of its existence, much less that of the universe. Science tries, but that is all that it can do. The problem remains.

So when one receives thoughts, he has to accept them without question. Memory, the association of thoughts, can be understood through experience, but for the ordinary person there is no way of transcending it.

In order to continue evolution of abstract thought, though, one has to understand himself.

There is no easy way to explain it except for saying that memory is life. For without memory, the life that we are used to would evanesce. Our jobs, character, experiences, house, children—all would be meaningless.

Alan relied on his memory. Peculiarly, it was as real to him as the floor he sat on, only if someone would have asked him to describe it, he couldn't. He understood his own insignificance, and tried to claw away every idea he had. He wanted to get away from everything. Be alone, like a child just born. He wanted to learn everything over again. It was a small price to pay, and he was full of volition to run away from it all as long as his present knowledge of himself, and the associations he possessed were expunged.

Two hours of loneliness passes. What can one think about before that time passes? Will thinking help make the horror run away quickly? No, not really, but there is really nothing else to do, and since it can't be avoided it is the only real thing that Alan has.

After going through some of the most constructive, and random thoughts he becomes a person of potential aid instead of one that is hated for his secrets. Surprisingly, someone who may have gladly killed him under different governing factors, now needs his relief. He is needed more now than ever because his help will seal a body of life draining wounds. In all this work he also manages to mend a friendship.

The sun shone throughout his ordeal. In the past, it was always present, even during the worst weather, above the clouds which shielded its glory—its undeserving beauty. People died, people were born, people were hurt all the while it shone, and continues to do so. It radiates its warmth regardless of the circumstances. It emits a truth that surpasses time. Its unspoken words painfully comfort the willing and humble body that accepts the eternal truth that has been presented it.

He wonders how he could ever have gone through the whole thing in one piece. Is there really anything to fear if he doesn't get killed? Is the fear real? Now considering . . . it isn't as much the wait that he fears as the backlash of events he thinks he will face once the determined hand of his captors will, once again, let the hurtful but honest bright light inside of his enclosure. It alarms him to think that it might be the last time he will be able to see any illumination whatsoever. That is the fear, and even if nothing comes out of it, it is enough to be real. There is nothing superficial about the deep-seated imaginativeness of the mind's eye, clearly viewing its death.

*   *   *

Andrew shut the door, and let Alan's thoughts run with, and blend into, the darkness enfolding him. He had a limited amount of time to decipher how to continue living.

He wanted to see every individual of his family again (even Robert). This was a problem because his perspicacity working in accord with his intuition, relative to a means of escape, was spasmodic. It came in short intervals of inspiration and even then the directive he received was askew. Precious thoughts came in pieces because they had to make leeway for the images that appeared of everyone he held dear to him.

His mind went like this: "maybe if I pretend that I am dead, my Liz looks beautiful in her wedding dress, I think that they might let me go free, Doug looks so cute starring at his first fallen out baby tooth . . ." Needless to say, he didn't get much accomplished. The result was that Alan was apprehensive, sentimental, and downhearted all at once. He needed focus.

Without warning the door to the clothes room abruptly opened. The butterfly of light fluttered into the darkness to prepare the prisoner for whatever was coming his way. It pulsated towards him with a speed that emphasized its urgency to communicate. It wiggled into his view by forcing his half shut eyes to look directly at it. Upon contact, the light rippled through his body like one gigantic wave on the ocean plane. Its power was there, but it tried to be gentle. It transformed the closet into a residence of salvation as it overtook and ruffled all of the darkness in it. Alan's thoughts occupied him so deeply that he didn't even cringe. He fell, like many victims, into a state of shock which helped him accept death. He didn't fear it. Everyone must die sometime; why does it matter. He trembled.

He awaited to see Andrew with weapon in hand pointing directly at his head brimmed with his usual malfeasance. He was no less surprised, though, when he saw Sanford. Either way, to him it meant the end. There was no way that they were going to let him go even if he told them everything that Luke had said. In fact, the truth was the only thing that kept him alive. Would they really kill him without finding out what they needed?

Sanford had come on a personal note without the others knowing. He convinced himself that his basic rudimentary instincts must have priority over his corrupted person.

The guilt that he felt for Randall was much weaker than the thoughts that had burdened Alan during the short period of isolation. Also, Sanford's will was very weak and he had to express any little prying weight upon his soul. He couldn't keep anything inside him.

"Alan," he whispered, "I have a job for you. You are the last chance that I have."

Alan saw the man's eyes. They were full of passion—indeed passion so extreme that he looked like a mad man on the verge of lunacy. It is no wonder that such a person could ever come into agreement to work with people as corrupt as Vincente and Andrew.

"You must help Randall. You realize . . . ." He stopped and became quiet as if he just came to a realization of the meaning of life. He frantically looked around the ground momentarily holding his eyes on random objects such as a stack of papers, brushes, pieces of wood, anything that lay on the floor of the closet that might help him think better.

Alan saw something very different about Sanford. He had completely changed. At times he acted normally, but there were occasions during which expressed the untamed spirit that Alan now saw visible in his eyes.

More importantly, Alan saw that his chance of escape rested with this man. He knew him well enough to understand that his mind was fragile enough to manipulate. He only needed time and the convenience of Andrew's and Vincente's absence—two things that he thought he would never get. Little did he know that he didn't need to exert any effort on his own. He was practically given the opportunity he sought.

"I never wanted him to get shot," he continued.

"You want ta know somethin'. Last year I went huntin', and I shot a Golden Retriever instead of a turkey." He just sat down and smiled at Alan. Alan, shocked and yet indifferent about the transformation in his friend, forced himself to return the smile. "My ninety eight year old mamma, though cooked it anyway. We had a feast . . . we did . . ."

"I thought that this was going to be simple you know that. You know me. Shakily he repeated, "I never wanted . . . ." They are going to kill him I know that. I told him to fake death. I think he can't do that for very long, especially since it is becoming real. Real!"

"You must get some help for him."

"How?"

"Run."

This man was an idealist. More realistically, though, he was a crackpot. Alan couldn't promise anything, but he wasn't in the position to make assurances. He was in a position to free himself, but he persuaded Sanford that he would do it, and felt like he was a doctor giving a Hippocratic Oath. He was ready to say anything just to run.

"You've got to hit me now."

"What?"

"That's right. It always works out this way. They are outside now thinking about what to do. They told me to watch you for a minute, but they won't expect that I helped you if ya clobber me."

His character changed again. Now he appeared to Alan as a plainclothesman—a policeman undercover as a civilian to protect the welfare of others.

"They don't trust me. You have to do it now."

Alan got out confident that his buddy wouldn't give him away, and ran to the small window near the ceiling. He praised God, pulled off the bars, hit Sanford with an alloy weight, and ran, not really sure where, to seek help.

He ran on a small road that lead all the way to the city.

This road was dilapidated and there probably were plans to restore it. Alan in many ways was like his son. They had mutual feelings in petty observations in life, but they never knew it because they never spoke of such subtle thoughts. They couldn't even be considered thoughts because they were so insignificant that they induced more of a feeling in the individual than any considerable pondering.

In any case, Alan loved to see the old pavement being conquered by sparse patches of crab grass. He didn't dwell over it, but simply loved to see it; just like some individuals love to see pictures of natural settings.

This is because there is a sense of peace, comfort, unity, and even order in something that man doesn't try to conquer. Nature is something that man has to live in accordance with while not trying to find it inferior to the human civilization.

This seemingly trivial image of the broken down road brought great ecstasy to him. That was why he chose it over the other roads. He couldn't think about it in depth when he did it because it was at the spur of the moment, but this instinct showed his natural tendency and attraction toward the environment which was expressed from his subconscious mind.

For Alan the road was a battlefield slowly being infiltrated by the deserving and exemplary. Ever since Alan could remember, he had a fascination with the concept of objects returning to the earth from which they came. Something as strong as asphalt will never outlast time, and eventually nature takes over in the weakest and most gentle way such as with the grass. Whenever there is some disaster inflicted upon nature by man, nature seems to be laughing inside. It plays with mankind knowing it will always be the winner since everything must return to its basic foundation anyway.

The fascination for Alan originated from his thoughts about life. It was remarkable to him that a truck, tank, or even a huge skyscraper would one day disintegrate into almost nothingness. It seemed as if all the human labor that extracted the iron ore from the mines and which produced machinery in the factories was unavailing, and useless. It brought a feeling of depression which often resulted in setting a dispirited mood, but at the same time he felt a warm comfort deep inside him eating away at this depression.

He knew that one day the sun would destroy the world when it would use up all of its fuel. Even more mind blowing was the thought that the universe itself would collapse on itself and all the matter would come together resulting in colossal destruction as all matter is reduced to the molecular level under the enormous pressures created by gravity. Did this mean that all the horrendous things that man has done will one day be meaningless? If so, wouldn't there be a down side to this which implies that all the successes that man has had will someday be completely extraneous to universal existence?

There were no answers. He couldn't think about it then. All that he had was a feeling of comfort walking on a road that would someday turn to dirt or even nothingness. In the past he had wondered why? Now he knew that some things weren't meant for men to figure out. He needed his sanity, and he needed to accept life, and enjoy his existence without worrying.

He lived life as Doug had before his transformation. He took it literally—not seeing God every direction in which he turned. Nature all around him was too vast and diverse to have evolved from a chemical pool years ago. God was everywhere, but he just couldn't see Him.

God directs people's lives, and through their ignorance of existence He comforts them in the most distressing of times. All He asks for is faith: faith in Him, His glory, and love. With these beliefs one then urges to satisfy and please God by abiding to His word.

Environment distracts people just as it did for Alan. Meaninglessness creates anger and frustration which disguises the ever searched for truth.

By the time he reached the city, he had calmed down, and walked into, what resembled, an old estaminet-like café to relax while being alert and cautious of his surroundings, thinking of home. He spoke to the public safety officer in the city through an anonymous call that he made from the café. He gave him directions to the building he thought he would die in and said that a murder occurred there. He left the MMI shortly afterward.

A few hours later he spoke with Evan whom he knew very well. This man had an extensive background in computer programming and he alone brought Alan out of this emerging crises.

Since Andrew knew that Alan was alive, Alan had to disappear, along with his family, and change his identity. Evan gave him a new name, hacked into the NAST supercomputer, which he always had access to, and transferred Alan under his new name to the underwater lab division. It was a great sacrifice his family had to make, but there wasn't really any other option open to them. It would have been very difficult for any of Andrew's conspirators to locate him successfully.

As for Andrew, Alan knew that he bypassed the ruling hand of the law and reestablished himself as the main agent provocateur of NAST. This man was much too cunning to be beaten by one man alone.

If anything commendable could be withdrawn from this wrecked and altered lifestyle, it was the bond that was reestablished between Alan and his devoted family. Rob was reconciled, and received the forgiveness that was given with much difficulty. It didn't mean that they never were as close as this or that they had somehow before lost this love, but that they sometimes didn't pay as much attention to it as they should have. They took it for granted, and paid more attention to things and events that were much less important.

They all knew that they depended on each other and that they had to live as a whole to be contented, but in the past they were afraid to show it too much.

There was a certain superficial comfort even arrogance behind being independent that showed everybody else that families are nice to have, but that they are an asset, something that tags along in life just to make it interesting. For some people in Alan's family this was more true than others. Rob was at the extreme side bordering an unconstrained and self-reliant lifestyle while Liz was on the other extreme end proclaiming the need for unity.

Everyone, no matter how much they loved another individual in their relations, camouflaged the expression of this love to some amplitude. Only when they all, as a family, were forced to alter their lifestyles together did they realize that the most meaningful thing that they had in the world was each other. They dropped their false faces and showed each other what they truly felt. This unleashing of human greed and evil, that created turmoil within the lives of four people, in the end helped Alan realize that the attachment his family had for him was always there, but now he was fond of it because they all were able to be themselves in front of him.

❖ *Chapter Seventeen* ❖

"She's just a little girl. Why is this happening now?"

Her parents loved her, and they would have done anything for her, but it was a bad time. She dreamt about the future, seeing visions of a family, having someone to love, holding in her arms a little son or daughter, and living in a beautiful house. This was normal, and the abnormality all around her was threatening the reality of these visions coming true.

How could anyone destroy this purposely? How could they take someone's hopes and dreams and destroy them in an instant with little or no remorse? At least if the targeted person was involved in and somehow muddied their hands in the politics of greed. Then the retaliation could be justified as deserving revenge, but innocent people should be in no position to suffer because of a dispute that they played no part in.

The house was small, and sat in an industrial covered belt which was surrounded by brown clouds of impurity. The families which were the originators, creators, and essential building blocks that established this district hadn't met with such defilement and contamination when they first moved there. There were, of course, other places to live, but this was the most suitable because little travel was necessary for vocation.

The pollution came gradually over the years so it wasn't really noticed until windows were beginning to get blackened by exhaust fumes, people were getting cancer from the water supply, and numerous cases of asthma and cardiac arrests became prominent throughout the area. From a distance the city of Chicago looked like a black hole in the earth into which sunlight refused to enter.

It was a bad time, but things got worse. It was bound to happen sooner or later. A détente between nations was something that could happen only after much fighting. It was unlikely to come any time sooner, no matter how much this poor little girl prayed for it. When the day finally came, and the previously unmoving smog had now given way to the dust and rubble thrown up into the air by random bombings, she prayed daily for something to make it all go away. She kept these prayers and wishes silent because she once heard that that was the only way that they would be fulfilled. The only emotions that she showed expressed themselves as tears in her mother's arms.

She had to suffer for another seven years with the loss of some very dear people to her. People just can't end something that they put so much effort into starting. There is a certain glory in going to war . . . getting ready for combat, saying goodbye to loved ones, feeling proud that a country believes in you.

What does it really mean? It means that after the pride and strength and belief in immortality are gone a mother has to come to grips with the fact that her country has exchanged her son for a death certificate; a piece of paper which resembles nothing else except the memories of a past life nicely bound up on a single page.

Liz had to exchange her brother for one of these messages. She didn't remember him too much because she was young and he was rarely home, but she did remember the feeling she got when she had to accept his passing. She never wanted to see the memories of anyone close to her ever bound up on such a piece of paper. She didn't need that because she had all the thoughts that she needed, and she could access them at will whenever she wanted. She didn't need some paper to remind her of what she already knew.

Her parents loved classical music, and Liz remembered that Souvenir de Florence: Adagio cantabile e con moto by Tchaikovsky was playing the moment the first bomb stuck. Outside the window, there was a huge flash of light followed by small pieces of bright glitter falling some ways off out of the sky. The distant images of small houses in the background (above the awning-like canopy of the trees in front of her house) that under normal conditions, even on a sunny day, were barely visible, now ceased to exist. In their place was a mountain of fire. The only consolation that she had was the protection and safety that the distance between the explosion and her house provided. This protection, though, only came from the fire that she saw and not from the source of that fire. For a few seconds later another explosion took place approximately midway between the former one and her own house.

This told her parents only one thing: to grab their children and run into the basement. All it had was some boxes, and a blackened light bulb that refused to die despite much use. Its entrance was under the carpet in the living room where a tiny square in the ground no bigger than three square feet hid the alcove that could fit no more than five people comfortably. It wasn't really a basement, but somewhat of an unfinished cellar. The people that designed the house originally planned for a basement, but never got it finished and this was the result. It was a good storage area, but also provided some protection from the world.

The last two blasts that they heard hit near the front of the house and about a mile from the back. They still remained unharmed.

During the next few days they had to face fires which threatened to take everything that they had ever owned. Their neighbor's house burned down, but the lack of high winds saved their own dwelling.

It wasn't easy living in a damp, dusty, and dark room. At times Liz felt like a contortionist because she had to make room for the storage of food but she didn't complain.

The aerial attacks continued. Long range missiles, whose flight was planned accurately by foreign supercomputers, caused most of the damage. The US military was initially at a loss to compete with all the fronts that threatened its borders. Maybe with some allies it would have been an easier war to fight.

Luckily the attacks on Chicago didn't last too long and Liz and her family returned to living relatively normal lives. The war still continued in many parts of the country though. Mostly US troops fought to contain the disasters in the US, and tried to prevent further ones by counteractions overseas.

One day a small group of fifty soldiers were ready to give up their lives in killing innocent people. All public safety buildings were demolished in the explosions and people now had to defend themselves. Liz saw two soldiers about six feet tall going into random houses and shooting defenseless families. These weren't foreigners because no foreign power was crazy enough to send ground troops onto US soil.

These were militia men who were stationed close to the Chicago area and their anti-patriotic beliefs fueled their hatred against their own country. It seemed as if they waited for such an opportunity, too long, to test their weapons and skills on others.

Only one thing forced humans to act like this. That force was hunger; a hunger to gain assets, justice, reputation, and power. The motivations for fighting weren't necessarily correct, morally, but a personalized belief in their morality was all that they needed to influence people to kill.

These people, upon showing their nature to all of their victims, were more than individuals of a corrupted militia. They were psychotic and deranged beings whose minds were too weak to resist the propaganda that they exposed themselves to.

In this war, Liz not only lost her brother, but both of her grandparents who were staying with her the moment the first bomb was dropped. Her grandfather was outside when the explosion startled him. He dropped to the ground and fell down the outside stairs. Her grandmother on the other hand could never have made it for her heart was way too weak.

Liz still thinks about what happened thirty-eight years ago by calling upon the moments of sadness, anger, despair, and loneliness to ease the severity of the events.

❖ *Chapter Eighteen* ❖

He was able to perceive what other people thought and it bothered him. Not that he didn't like to feel and almost hear in his head what other people thought or to finish their sentences for them, but what bothered him about it was that he didn't know why it was happening or even how. It wasn't in any of the books that he read and it certainly wasn't common knowledge on which he could get advice from others on.

Most of all, his changed person wasn't limited to thinking the thoughts that other people had. Each one of his five senses improved. He received a great sensitivity in his fingers. So great that he could feel the painted colors of objects.

His hearing improved to that of a bat, and at night for fun he would make clicking noises with his mouth just so he could practice on identifying all the objects in the room and their locality according to his own position. Once he felt confident that he knew where many of the objects were he would roll over to his side and continue the same procedure until he created a new mental picture of the world to the right of him. He was able to tell what kind of objects stood just a few feet away from him by their relative size and density.

He assumed that this great perception of his environment was due somehow to his ability to receive the sound waves (that he emitted from his mouth by clicking his tongue against his upper teeth) that were bounced off the objects in the room. Depending on the hardness of the material the received wave would have a larger or smaller period, and he became able to distinguish the differences in pitch that they produced.

This was freaky for him. He didn't think that the human mind could distinguish between such fine differences in sound. To test his limits he would walk around at night making this sound and seeing if he could navigate his way through his room.

His sight was yet another improvement. In the past his right eye was weaker than his left. Now he was able to focus both eyes together or separately, whenever he wanted, and on anything. He felt like a robot able to adjust to his environment perfectly with almost no effort.

His taste and smell improved in magnitude just as much as his other senses.

Since such high sensitivity was limited to extremely sensitive scientific devices no one really believed him when he spoke of his abilities. He had to prove himself, and the amazement he received was well worth it. People began to hear of this talented boy and would stop by occasionally to give him a few tests. Generally, these people were friends, and he was cautious not to brag to much to too many people.

The realization of this change came all of a sudden. He figured that he had these gifts for some time but that he just wasn't aware of them. Only when he had some time alone to think was he able to discover what he possessed.

One day he felt good about what he had and it didn't really bother him anymore that he didn't know where or why he got these talents. He just wanted to use them to impress people and to show his hidden superiority over them. Most of all he wished that he could show the people he used to hang out with: Slick Willy, Dirk, Big Pete, Raymond, and Anthony. In this regard, Doug had a very competitive nature that he couldn't control. This was because it controlled him, and he loved it.

Meditation brought it out in him. Before he learned how to meditate he knew that it was important to be modest and that he had to treat others as he himself wanted to be treated. There was some supervenient quality in him that questioned these characteristics, though, and always was the rebel part of his being. He wondered why, now. Why was it so important to care about others when you could belittle their weaknesses and feel good about yourself in the process?

It didn't matter, he got a high out of showing off, and if that made him happy, he wasn't going to change for some worn-out phrases demanding the respect of others whose origins were as dubious as their words advocating courtesy.

The arrival at HYTRE675F marked a watershed in the history of Doug's life. He had plenty of time for himself. He didn't want to go to school. He didn't want to work, but his parents said that they needed the help because they both received cuts in their salaries. When there would be something available for a high school graduate, they would jump at the opportunity.

Until then Doug spent his days walking through the facilities that were open to the families of employees. He went on a few tours, and saw numerous labs with much equipment. These labs were simple and contained very basic contrivances. Many of them weren't used anymore and served just as storage rooms filled with devices that might be of interest to some. He saw the lithology lab which was used as one of these storage rooms holding densimeters, alkalimeters, actinometers, acidimeters, flasks, beakers, and even broken old multitasking computers and analytical engines which could probably now be put to no better use than as a door stop somewhere.

All the highly sophisticated labs were closed to the non-scientists excepts for the psephology one. The study of electrons was considered to be old news since no new research has come out concerning them. Supposedly, they had been investigated to their fullest. Doug liked that one the most, though, and wished that he could have had some time alone to study the provisions with which the government had supplied NAST.

Eventually, he got board of these tours, and waited in his room looking out into the ocean through one of the horizontally positioned skylights nearest to him. He didn't get amused anymore with gadgets and technology.

He thought of his home below the ever towering Hunter Mountain, and wished that he could go back just to see it for a few days with Old One Eye running around him. He never wanted to give that dog away. Sometimes his consciousness matched that of a human, and Doug felt it in the look that only his dog could give him.

So he went back to his old hobby of meditating. Only this time the quiet around him aided his concentration. The sound of bubbles outside, the noise of an incoming vessel finished with the exploration of the plates; finished with gathering enough samples of the ocean floor for the creation of new fuel.

This environment and the technique that he acquired over the years with practice promoted his urge to develop his mind as much as he could. He felt a strong energy here, and it was enough to do what he heard about before: to focus the energy of the mind like a magnifying glass onto one thought and therefore make the mind frighteningly powerful. He concluded that he must have been feeling such mental strength because he has been keeping up with his exercises.

Once he was convinced of his mental strength he tried to translate it in a physical power. During one circumstance he picked up a metal bar, made from an admixture of metals, used to close the main doors during an emergency by rotating huge circular wheels manually. This bar wasn't very thick but it had to be strong. He was curious if he could bend it. After all it wasn't huge. He grabbed it with both hands and started to exert all the energy that he could. On top of this he imagined that he had the strength of a tank in his hands. Every time that he started to shake his body he realized that he was trying too hard and was losing his focus. So he took a deep breath, hands still clenched with all their might on the bar, and relaxed his upper body so that he got his breathing back to normal. The only tension in his body was at his hands and shoulders. The rest was in complete peace. He eased away the tension like this a couple of times while increasing it where he wanted it. He closed his eyes the whole time. When he felt that he had enough he stopped—just like that. When he looked at his hands he was rather surprised to see that they were black and blue and covered in blood, and that he didn't feel any pain whatsoever. Even more surprising to him was that the bar had yielded under his stress and became plastically and permanently deformed. The bending was slight, but it was obvious.

The concept of meditation changed many times. For Doug, it meant an escape from the world. He knew that it held power, but he also knew that he had to channel it usefully.

The only way to change the feelings he had in the past was to live every moment consciously aware of who he wanted to become. The regret of the past didn't matter. It would have only upset him. He rejoiced at the conscious rediscovery of his free will.

Its was a shame. His whole live was wasted, unless he wasn't ready yet to learn from it, because he was unsuspecting—unbelieving. He veered erroneously. Free will is as much a savior for wrongdoing as it is an odyssey of piety.

He told his parents what had happened when they asked about his hands, but they didn't believe him. They made up some possible tale for the bar being bent which Doug thought was more fantastic than the truth. He claimed he could do it again. They didn't want to hear any more.

He started reading books and got board after he didn't encounter anything challenging. Despite his power to control the amount of concentration at will he wanted to commit towards some project, he still didn't feel blissful. He felt as if he needed an ablution of his body which was being continuously defiled by something, the source of which he didn't understand.

He needed help. He was like someone just discovering the power hidden inside every single molecule of every object only to be destroyed by his discovery of how to release that energy. He was on to something, and strangely was in control and yet out of control. He didn't doubt for a second that if he tried hard enough and maybe used more than twenty percent of his brain in concentration that he would be able to move objects freely around with his paranormal inclination. Maybe he was insane, maybe he just wasn't normal, or maybe he was just interested in parapsychology.

The only person with whom he could freely talk about this issue was Herbert. Would it be hapless to seek contact with a religious fanatic again? Just then he got an urge to read *Nevesta Kristova*, the book that his brother had gotten from Manya in Picin. He didn't know why he thought of that now. He couldn't even read the book. Why would he want to look into it?

Just then he remembered that Herbert wrote down a way to contact him on a shredded segment of a newspaper, and that this scrap of paper was possessed by that book alone which he had placed there a while ago. His mind was better than he had thought.

After speaking to Herbert, they both decided upon a meeting place. This was, of course, on land and it meant that Doug would have to sneak away for a few hours. He thought about telling his parents, but since they really never met either Herbert or Isabelle he was almost certain that they wouldn't let him go.

There was the danger that somehow Andrew might find out about Alan and somehow try to kidnap their son in order to get back at him for retreating from the MMI. Doug thought that the risk was exonerated of its possible mishaps as he climbed into the shuttle which visited the solid earth above every two days. This was still another attraction for the families in the underwater lab to avoid boredom.

On the ground bordering the ocean from which he emerged like some mythical monster sentenced to a life of isolation by the Gods he saw the cofferdams built along the shorelines in the distance. It wasn't enough for people to have huge underwater labs. They had to build more and more. It was the human way. These cofferdams were huge walls built in the ocean bordering the shore so that water could be pumped out from within their walls. This enabled workers to build structures underwater with ease and then upon completion of the structures let the water back in to surround them.

Doug had a strange feeling. It looked funny to see huge gaps in the ocean. From the distance where he stood it seemed like the Earth had provided some unnatural barrier in the shape of a square to prevent water from touching the dry ground. It looked like an art picture. Something that should never have existed. In any case he didn't want to ponder over the anomalous picture. He was happy to feel the sun and breeze on his skin. He realized how much he had really missed it.

The house of worship that Doug walked into was fairly small. He was surprised that he had found it only with the little map that he bought of the area. It was near an old school off a small road and tolerably isolated, meaning that there was some development around it, but not too much. It looked like a very old chapel. Possibly it was built in the late nineteenth century and rebuilt many times since then as time wore away its history.

He walked over the broken tiles that served as a welcoming path positioned in front of two broad, heavy, and nicely carved oak doors that made up the main introgression. They both squeaked at the hinges as he opened them.

Inside, the chapel was timeless. It probably hadn't changed at all for the last fifty years. The floor was all wooden. Next to the entrance on the right stood a dainty chair made out of beach, the legs of which were roughly nailed together. It served as an attraction, but Doug guessed that no one could ever sit on it who is used to living in luxury. On the left stood another chair that was more ornately designed, but still seemed to be hand made. It was characterized by a wickerwork of interlaced osiers, and twigs, and it was astonishing that someone could have such determination to create something so delicate. Above these two chairs was the donation box and a small bowl nailed to the wall which held some holy water.

There was a note on a small table that immediately told Doug that Herbert was in the basement or some sort of undercroft of this church. This subterranean room wasn't a vaulted chamber, even though that may have been its primary purpose.

Upon entering this sepulchral region of the church, Doug saw that it wasn't gloomy or repulsive. It had an elegance to it that wasn't quite matched by some of the other areas of the church. Herbert who was near a lamp looking at some of the designs on the wall turned around abruptly when he heard the presence of another being in the room.

"Oh Hi. You startled me."

He pointed his finger in the direction of his observation.

"Beautiful. Isn't it?"

Ever since Doug met Herbert, he felt comfortable around him. He didn't feel the need to observe any punctilio. He could act anyway that he pleased.

"Oh Yes. Very much so."

While talking to him at that instant, Doug saw him not as a deeply spiritual person, but as a pundit and a critic of beauty.

"I don't think that we should be here, but I am not doing anything bad. It is a shame that people don't come here anymore."

He was right. He wasn't doing anything bad, but Doug was still surprised that he would venture around in the church as if it were he who had built the place.

They walked up to the first level, and right out through the immense doors to talk. They walked slowly, but they were covering distance, so absorbed were they in thought.

Doug started the conversation by telling him the true reason why he needed to seek his company. He was having a spiritual crises, and he was afraid that he was falling into the swank and egotistic display of preeminence that he witnessed in the shed with Will Simmons close to his home in New York.

He told him that he never felt so powerful and yet likewise he never felt so miserable and ungratified. He wished that he could reverse the effects of meditation, but whenever he tried not to think about it he was only fooling himself.

They walked around on a parking lot which headed off into some ornamental planting, underbrush, and sparse trees which were part of a once dazzling park. Now the scenery looked like it had been glossed over by the people that used to go there, as if they deliberately chose to ignore it. It was precious, though, like a book attentively holding knowledge ready for a willing person to open and enjoy it. People were no longer interested in the outdoors.

Herbert told Doug that people might seem lost, but they do it to themselves because they are afraid of the uncertainties they have in being found by something that they cannot understand. He told Doug that he could make a big difference in the world if he gives some thought to his own existence.

Much of what he told him didn't make sense. To Doug, it was like a lot of nonsense from some philosophy book or some magical manual for life that spoke of reasoned doctrines, metaphysics, logical concepts, epistemology, critical studies and ethics.

This man was here to help him, but all he accomplished doing was to make him more confused. Maybe it was an error to come to him.

Doug didn't have to say a word because Herbert saw his torment.

Herbert nudged him on the shoulder, "You should say something if you are confused."

He continued to speak of God and life, but this time it was all very clear. He stated that this was the way that he saw things, and that they didn't necessarily have to conform to any particular group of people. Though he prayed with groups, he held strong personal beliefs which gave him the insight that Doug lacked.

He told him the limits of his reasoning. God advocates love and every one of his creations cries out for this love. This is basic. What makes it so hard for the common individual to pray for his neighbor in times of need, give money to the impecunious people in the world, and generally love complete strangers is that people have been exposed to some source of evil and vice during their development. If this wouldn't have happened then there wouldn't be any reason why people should lose the innocence that they were born with. Greed, the struggle for power, the enjoyment of seeing others down all corrupt our beings, but these paths to evil are followed because they bring temporary enjoyment. They assuage the troubles in the world and make the common individual who sees love disintegrating before him embrace the force that causes this disintegration. Humans are meant to be so spiritual that they can't bear witness to see the world fall apart, but because there are also those without faith who have too weak a will to fight the injustices they see, they promote them instead. These people can never be truly happy.

The purpose of life is to follow your feelings. It couldn't be stated simpler. To follow the feelings that you as a child had when you weren't corrupted by any other individual, is to be on the path towards betterment. The second half of the purpose of life on earth as viewed by Herbert is for each individual to use the foundation he possesses of understanding what is right or wrong by what he feels and sees around him and apply logic and reason to it. Upon coming to the age when people can see an event occur in the world and think about whether it is just or not, they begin to break away from the trap that many others have fallen into. The next step is to carefully distinguish between sincerity and hypocrisy.

The following example illustrates hypocrisy. If an individual is approached with some horrible news and is told that someone has passed away, the individuals first reaction is to worry about family, and loved ones. If truth reveals that it was the death of a neighbor, then there might be some relief present which tells the individual's consciousness "Thank God that it wasn't anyone that was close to me." This hypocrisy illustrates that there exists a lack of compassion and empathy towards strangers or acquaintances that isn't quite true for family and loved ones.

The barrier that must be crossed is to love everyone, and try to be the best that any individual can be without comparing himself or herself to others. Once this is done people become confident in themselves because they know that they aren't out to hurt anyone. They don't get worried about finances or others because they know that worrying doesn't do anything positive; it only builds stress. Besides there is no need for worry because when someone knows that he is trying very hard to succeed in life with business, or love, worry is only something extra that isn't needed.

When people succeed in following these guidelines, there is still room for them to fall from grace. Money causes arrogance and a feeling that if I can achieve this I must be better than you. Once this thought comes into someone's head they break the rule of loving others. They might feel temporarily happy that they have hurt someone, but it will come back to them and hit them hard. They will lose satisfaction and ease of living and their perceptions will get clouded with worse thoughts. They will be bothered by it or they will think of other ways to hurt people and this distraction created by their loss of focus is enough for them to lose their success.

To change one's life to such an extent as to follow two simple rules (love others, and be the best that you can) takes enormous discipline. It requires an individual, constantly, to think of the way he lives life and whenever an action is made he has to think whether it harmonizes with his purpose on earth. In cities and other places of distraction on the globe, it is laborious to come up with this type of lifestyle all alone. That's is why people take religious journeys into the depths of solitude to sort out their perplexing thoughts.

Once, however, change comes around the person can be considered enlightened. Nothing will bother him, and better yet there is no way that he could be hurt by others because he realizes that they are simply lost and that he has found himself. He doesn't think he is better because everyone is ignorant of the origins of life on earth, but awareness of this fact is all that he needs. The enlightened individual will achieve a tremendous focus because no thoughts will be distracting him, and his inner person, dictating what is correct, will be in harmony with his actions, and conscious thoughts. This leaves more time to focus on work.

This calmness is what Doug saw in Herbert and what made him want to talk to him. He had to learn from him just so that he could find out where he got his confidence from. After their talk Doug realized that he has been miserable because he hadn't followed his rules.

No wonder he felt irritable. There was great reason for this since his thoughts kept on going towards his actions of superiority which he gained through meditation. His feelings told him that something was wrong and his subconscious mind wouldn't let him be happy.

Now he understood, and felt a relief that he could get help on such a difficult issue. There was still much work and self-control to be done, but this would come with time as long as he knew what he wanted.

Herbert concluded by saying that there was no reason that people shouldn't follow this way of life. If they felt that it was ludicrous and insipid then they didn't realize that they have nothing to lose. Everyone dies, and even the universe doesn't last forever. Life can't be composed of living wildly for the moment, instead one should live a controlled, happy, and enlightened existence knowing that nothing that is done can hurt anyone else. This feeling of worthiness perpetuates itself to others just as it should.

To those who can't see, God is a mystery. Those who are able to comprehend his grace have unlimited vision into universal truism.

Herbert didn't speak eternal truths. They were words of Doug's life. Imperfect falsification was a helmsman to impartiality.

❖ *Chapter Nineteen* ❖

From where did Herbert get his insights to life?

His childhood wasn't very salubrious. He was a rather weak child and smaller than many others the same age as himself. Customarily, he was sick and didn't get out as much as he would have liked because he was forced to recuperate in bed. Much of his mental anguish was translated into signs that worsened his physical condition. His psychosomatic life was protracted by the other children that, when he was well and could go outdoors, jeered at his pale and sickly appearance.

Also, diabetes didn't allay this hard life of his. He was talking many drugs which helped lower his blood sugar levels, but no drug could have taken away the haunting memories that other children had impressed upon his mind.

This used to bother him so much that without really thinking about a situation he would pick fights with whoever insulted him. He got started on a downward spiral which he couldn't easily avoid. His losses in many of the fights depressed him even more, but his stay at home requiring the recovery of a broken arm, or leg served as an enlargement of his capabilities for animosity.

He inherited one thing that ruined his life tremendously. That was insecurity. He had it as long as he could remember and as much as he fought it, it just wouldn't go away. It was frustrating because he didn't have the control to guide the life he wanted. So he fought his fear and vacillation by trying to beat others. He knew that he wasn't strong enough to beat himself.

Once there was this child who was much taller than he was. This child had his own group of friends and he was so cruel that others didn't even want to be caught in his presence. The day that Herbert met with him, this bully, after attacking him with incisive words, picked him off of the ground while his buddies frisked Herbert and stole all his money. Instead of being afraid, he got angry, but he thought that this wouldn't have been the best time to express it.

So, his response was to fight dirtily. One thing that Herbert was proud of was his arm. He could throw a mean fast ball. Whenever he was alone he would practice throwing baseballs behind his house. He waited for this bully, Ox as they all called him, to come outside after school. Herbert picked the perfect place to hide behind some low shrubs. When he saw his enemy's back about twenty feet away he yelled his name through the bushes. His confused expression is all that he saw and remembered as the rock he had thrown flew directly into it, breaking his nose. The sidewalk slowly became colored red drop by drop as Ox bent over holding his nose. He could hit his target again, he thought, and released the second round which struck the top of his head sending him to his knees.

The shot was perfect. Herbert never doubted himself because he felt so sure that he would succeed that he never hesitated. The vision in his head matched and even seemed inferior to what had actually happened.

Ox never saw Herbert do this because he was looking in a different direction through the crowds of children from which he though he heard his name called. The children that did see the act of intrepidity and fearlessness didn't say a word to anyone because they were grateful.

He continued to fight others in this manner, though not always using rocks. Sometimes he would kick people before the fight started or injure them some way the day before they were to fight so that the next day he was proclaimed victor through default.

His parents became more shocked than cross when they heard about their son's behavior from school. They didn't think that their son could ever hurt someone else.

They were deeply religious people whose Jewish background had always taught them to treat others with impartiality and love. They decided to restrict their son's free time which he spent as they thought being corrupted by others. They imposed stricter religious practices on him. If anything, this would bring him to a realization of a different purpose in life.

It did change his life, but not as much as his parents had wished. He was too young to understand the deep implications of what his religion truly meant, and he couldn't take it as seriously as they did. His only reward was the satisfaction that he saw on the faces of others who were convinced that he was really trying to study the theology he was presented with.

During these times his life was filled with a longing for something he couldn't find. He didn't even know what it was, but he knew that he wasn't happy. There were three paths of his life that converged at a focus of his uncertainty. They were always tearing him apart from being one person and asked for him to act differently in different occasions. One led to the great, but temporary, power he felt in hurting another person. The second led to religious wisdom through a thorough examination of the religious teachings to which his parents had introduced him. The third path was his own judgment. It was built by his mind and it told him what was right or wrong from the previous two paths. The reason this was a separate path in itself and not one that directed the other two is because he couldn't always listen to himself. Sometimes before he was about to hurt a person he knew that it was wrong but the power that that path for the time being provided in leading his life was too great for him to overcome. In short, he didn't have enough control to avoid the emotions that were ripping apart his mentality and disengaging his being by defocusing his energies onto the triaxial paths of his awareness.

Then came the day when his life everlastingly changed. One morning he was having a pain in his stomach. It was slight, and he tried to disregard it especially since he was taken to a doctor who said that it was all in his mind. He went to school, but it got worse. His pain was so bad that if he hadn't seen the nurse he felt as if his insides would have torn him apart. The nurse immediately sent him to the hospital where he later met his parents.

His appendix had burst and there was a great chance that he would die. The surgeons didn't waste any time.

During surgery he had received too much anesthetic. Death came slowly and painfully. Then in a moment it was welcome. The crippled body which from above barely touched the pure white covers suffered no more.

At first he was hovering above it and saw everything that the doctors had been doing. He saw objects that would have been out of his range of vision had he been fully conscious.

He was frightened. It was all so real to him that he didn't even regard it as a dream. It was as if he had full consciousness, and perception of everything he saw.

A moment later a tunnel of light had opened up in front of him and he felt attracted to it. Inside the light he had a feeling of absolute peace and security. Most of all he felt that he was loved.

It all lasted such a short time; not longer than a few minutes. He wished that he could stay there forever and he never wanted to leave. He was sure that more was intended; something more that could be added to his peace, but he wasn't exposed to it.

Almost instantly he was back hovering above his body. Then darkness. The peace out of grasp brought back his emptiness. If only it would have stayed. If only he knew how to keep it.

When he awoke in the intensive care unit, he told the nurses and doctors what had happened to him, but no one believed him. They all thought that he was having some delusion from the overdosed drug that they admittedly said was a major mistake on the part of the anesthesiologist.

During those brief seconds he knew he had had an extraordinary experience. People could have convinced him otherwise but he knew what had happened. Others around the world have had similar experiences and they all spoke of common feelings and events that characterize these out of body experiences. Many of them see their bodies below them, and see the tunnel of light just as Herbert had.

The increasing number of cases demonstrating supernatural experiences has lead the medical world to a slow and painful acceptance that life is made of more than science. For every cell that is observed by scientists and for every structure that lies within it that is identified and named, the puzzling questions that ask about its very existence remain.

There are many scientists who are still skeptical of these out of body experiences and seek a possible explanation using their knowledge of the human body, checking any possibility—anything that could offer the slightest solution to the uncertainties that they have to confront.

After it happened to Herbert, he saw life differently. He began to treat others with the peace he encountered. If they could have felt what he felt. If they could have gone through it, jealousy and hatred would mean nothing to them. He became more passive with bullies and accepted his condition in life. He didn't get angry and he didn't seek revenge. It seemed like a waste of his energy.

Before long his parents inquired about his genteel behavior. He couldn't make up some story so he told them, again, exactly what had happened. They told him to keep it to himself. A story like this couldn't get out into the open.

Unfortunately for them it did. It was inevitable. He told a few of his closest friends who thought that he finally went out of his mind, and soon almost everyone he knew had heard about it.

Word came around to his synagogue and he was an anathema for everyone there; someone devoted to evil; a cursed soul. He still felt the need to learn about his religion, but couldn't understand why people were so unwilling even to listen to him.

This was especially true of his parents. Whenever he started talking about what had happened they would begin to talk about something completely different. Once he got angry and said, "You all think I'm irrational, and probably wish that you had a normal son don't you."

Sure what he said sounded very far-fetched. He wasn't even sure if he could have believed such a story if someone had told it to him before his appendix burst, but he did expect more compassion.

It was difficult because people felt uncomfortable being around him. They didn't want to talk with him fearing that his mind would snap in front of them. "The years that he endured being teased finally caught up with him," was just one of the many excuses made up by his friends.

Every day he thought about ways to better himself. He wanted to show everyone that he met that there is more to life, much more. So far, he had frightened people. The way that he could express the love that he felt in the light was to treat every person that he met with the same love and kindness without getting in to too much detail about his death.

Since he was anathematized he had joined some spiritual cults, but couldn't find the same satisfaction that he had felt as he hovered above his body years ago. The experiences that he had in search of fulfilling his spiritual hunger had all left him equally, if not more hungry than before.

Until the day he met Doug he was wondering what he had to do to make his existence the most meaningful. Later on he knew that it didn't matter. As long as he loved everybody and had no ill feelings in him and focused his energies onto one path in life that only led to benignity and excellence there was no reason why he should pester the ignorance that he was meant to possess.

Doug became his pupil, not in the sense that he went to him to learn hard facts about life from old literature, but as an individual curious about what he had to offer life. It wasn't bad to learn from the bible or many other religious works. If anything it was beneficial and a different form of excellence, but Herbert's personal experience helped show Doug a different side to religion.

Herbert didn't have a religion, or at least not a specific one. What he had was a very broad understanding of life and he integrated it into a personal religion. It went like this: people could basically do whatever they want as long as love is present. They have to follow hidden blueprints in their minds which tell them to favor equality, harmony, justice, peace, and symmetry among the people. He didn't want to be part of any religion that corrupted these values or many others he held which were subcategorized by these main ones.

Some of the religions are always righteous in their ideals but it is the people that corrupt them. Corruption gives way for pardoners, for example, which were medieval preachers delegated to raise money for religious works by granting indulgences. For him, money doesn't pardon a person of the sins that he committed during a lifetime, and many people would agree with this. This is exactly what he wanted to tell others.

People feel for themselves what is right or wrong, and they don't need to follow set doctrines if they believe that they are incorrect.

All the religions in the world speak of the same or similar values that Herbert held. Herbert's long term goal was to show everybody that he met and was willing to listen to him that all the religions are equal in their messages and that the distinction between them shouldn't create a need to fight. Doesn't that go against the first law of loving others?

Members of different religions should accept each other's traits as a sign of the great diversity within humanity which shaped different means, but always held a unifying theme towards salvation. Herbert felt that God couldn't be pleased by seeing individuals provoke fighting and evil just because they couldn't accept diversity.

Most of all, Herbert enjoyed the talks that he had with Doug. He spoke about everything that he knew and theorized. He felt affined to Doug. There was some obligation he refused to deny that he had in forming this boy's image of the world so that he didn't lose his focus like he himself almost had before his accident.

Herbert thought well. His intentions were good. He might have been far from the truth about existence, but he tried to oppose evil whenever he could. After that one day, seeing the white sheets under him, when he felt the purity of confession he questioned no more.

Herbert was reformed.

❖ *Chapter Twenty* ❖

He was gone for now. If he was roaming the facilities out of boredom it would take, possibly, up to two hours to locate him. The area which he had access to was colossal.

After it had happened, they were feeling guilty because they told him that he could go anywhere he wanted, anytime, as long as he informed them of any distant trips. They didn't want to restrict what little happiness and pleasure he got from being investigative since he had lost so much as a part of the sacrifice he had to make. The worry, though, for them wouldn't go away and upon finding that he wasn't in their temporary home they started to panic.

Nothing could have really happened to him here. All the excuses that they had made up circled around this one thought. He was surrounded by security and safety.

It was common for them to take hold of ideas that brought them comfort. There was a good and bad side to everything, and they didn't want to attract any baneful or unfavorable events because of their thinking. It was time to be positive and hopeful. If positive thoughts made people happy then it was time to engage in what the optimistic lifestyle had to offer.

The truth was that any more abrogating news could have taken them down single-handedly. In spite of the strength of their love for each other, it was no match for one more disaster. It was enough to escape a threat of homicide, and see a best friend not as lucky, to want to complete a life of peace.

His absence, however, brought about clouds of doubt that hovered above the invulnerability that they had felt so confident about when they had initially arrived. It annihilated the hope for peace by demonstrating that comfort didn't eradicate a chance for trouble.

They were correct to be concerned.

*   *   *

Doug had thought about Herbert's discussion with him. He now knew what was right and wrong—he always had, in fact, but now he consciously lived by directing his life.

He didn't like being lost, but that is how he lived up till now. Even as he reached adulthood and all the respect that he anticipated with it, he felt that he had overlooked something that he desperately needed in the adult world.

He traipsed out of his room to see whether Herbert's insight was the missing component that filled the void he had acknowledged. The more he thought, the more he knew that he no longer traveled to infinity going on endless voyages, through never ending barriers, only to be interrupted by the sporadic false sense of reality. He didn't see this reality, that he for now was a part of, as false. It was real, very real, and Herbert gave it texture.

Love came to him in the next instant. It always existed, but by seeing it in a human form he felt it very strongly.

He walked down a brightly lit hallway and saw Susi walking straight towards him! He couldn't believe it. Was this really her? Why was she here?

This wasn't the same person he had maintained in his mind since he last saw her. Instead of a child, she looked like a thirty year old women who had plenty of life experience. She walked with an earnestness that matched that of other business women, including his mother, whom he had seen walk the halls of this subdivision of NAST. She lost the child-like joviality that had characterized her walk at the Neoteric Carnival Show they had seen together.

In her hands she grasped a box of computer diskettes, and while briefly looking up to make sure that she wouldn't run into anything, she managed to shuffle through them as if she had no time to lose. During one of those brief upward glimpses, her eyes met Doug's eyes. Doug was about to yell to her, but he saw that she didn't register him. Maybe she didn't recognize him because of the way that he looked or maybe because she just had too much on her mind.

As she almost walked by him, he grabbed her by the shoulder. She sharply looked up and he could see the shocked expression on her face partly covered by her long hair.

"Doug! I never thought that I would see you again," she said as she warmly hugged him.

Even though she was obviously in a hurry, she took some time to sit down in the closest vacant lecture room to talk.

She was a child again. In his arms the seriousness and mature persona, the world had imposed on her, departed. In a few seconds, memory let her change into a completely different person.

Doug told her that he wasn't able to write her because his whole family feared for their lives. He felt terrible that he couldn't even tell her of her father's death. He mentioned all that has happened since he saw her last.

As he spoke it didn't seem real. It seemed like he was talking about someone else's life. Maybe someone whom he had read about. Even he couldn't believe it all. He told her about Anthony, and his own close call with death, and his father's narrow escape. It was dangerous even to talk with her because Andrew might be watching her and using her as a bait to catch Alan or one of his family members.

"That's why we have changed our name," he said.

Then she asked him something that he was afraid to confront. "Tell me everything that you know about my father."

He wasn't prepared to go into details partially because he didn't want to hurt her, and partially because he didn't want to skew and contort the truth. Nonetheless, he told her all that Alan told him.

She hadn't known the truth about Luke's death until now. She and Ellen both received a message from the company that Luke had died on the job, and that everybody at work was expressing their deepest sympathies for the family.

Halfway through her explanation of the notification she began to cry. She didn't want to be hurt again.

She had to go, but promised that she would meet him in two hours after she was done with her work. They decided to meet in the lithology storage lab so as not to arouse suspicion.

It was conceivable that she was under Andrew's control, and always watched. Andrew knew that if Alan was Luke's friend then contact might be established with Susi some time in the future. It was dangerous to be even seen with her.

She had begun work in this sea laboratory because her stepmother was having fiscal problems without Luke. Susi found a job in the same department as her father had worked three months ago, and she found it strange that she hadn't run into Doug at all during that time. Both were living on the second level near the south shuttle.

The most disturbing news that he received was that Andrew was working two domes away. Evidently, he had moved there just recently as his promotion demanded that he relocate. As far as Doug knew he was making good money before. Now he has gone ahead of himself as he ranked among the most influential people controlling NAST. This was more than a promotion. It was an elevation almost to the complete top; an enhancement of greed and jealousy without regret. Doug was sure that he used his deceitful and crooked diplomacy to get there.

The people that he had stepped on couldn't do a thing about his job, and he made sure that all of the others that he secretly got rid of and overpowered were no longer alive to break his reputation of strength and admiration by an elite few who were too blind to see past his humble and gallant mask.

There was nobody who could stop a man like this with so much authority, and ingenious adroitness. Only Doug and his family could stand up to him and face his disrespectful nature. But only they knew the truth. Since they were in hiding and Alan nowadays just wanted to be left alone, it appeared that Andrew would remain unchallenged.

He had to tell his father at once what Susi had told him because there could always be the possibility of a chance encounter however unlikely it may seem. Someone might recognize him, a coworker, friends—anyone, and the news of his presence might, haphazardly, be delivered to Andrew.

Doug went back to his family's chambers waiting till two thirty so that he could see his love. He did what he got used to doing underwater: he slept a lot.

He couldn't meditate. He wasn't in the mood. He hadn't been for a while, ever since he spoke with Herbert. He just starred at his surroundings thinking about his life, and whatever images came into his mind. For once, during morning relaxation, he didn't try to control the stream of thoughts that naturally flowed in everybody.

In front of his eyes he saw the orange tree. It was beautiful. This was the only plant that he had taken with him from home. Four years ago he kept a seed from an orange he was eating. He threw it into a pot of soil that was occupied by a cluster of posies, just to try and see whether he would have any luck growing anything. Sure enough in a few days the organism started germinating. He was amazed upon the sight of its small leaves.

Over the years he had transplanted it several times. When he was supposed to move to the lab, he wanted some plant with him. It was perfect. It was as if it owned its life to him, and he in return felt an obligation to care for it. He had trimmed it before winter came every year regularly, and created somewhat of a bonsai. Now he waited for the fruits.

As he looked at it now it appeared to be withering under the artificial light never holding the promise of bearing fruit. Its needs were served by a nature manufactured by man. An imitated nature. One that could control the climate, light, water, and the soil containing nourishment that it clung to for its existence.

This intelligent and seemingly superior nature that evolved from the very nature it was trying to imitate could never surpass the macrocosm that created it. The attempts to do so result from a grieving knowledge of this reality. Therefore the attempts are discouraged by their creators before being discouraged by their creators' creator. Man will always have a knowledge of this failure.

Man tires to challenge his surroundings even though he knows that he could never beat them. People try to simulate and in a way surpass the nature around them, but it is all to little avail because they have to first be able to understand it and how it relates to their origins. Those who think that they have duplicated nature in a test tube should think about their declarations. Can their nature exist or undergo morphogenesis in their labs without their consistent stimuli. The answer is no. Nature is chaotic, and trying to make order out of something that demands ever increasing entropy results in folly. The only good that could come out of it is if it helps mankind. Any other reason such as demonstrating human genius and aptitude drowns in a small lagoon of mental arrogance which only separates man from his curiosity of and understanding with nature.

Doug woke up when he heard a message being left by some Mr. Michaels. It was an opportunity for a job—a very well paid job.

He got up and got appropriately dressed. He decided to see this man and check if there was any catch to the opportunity. He would surprise his parents later when he tells them that he got a position.

The abode was now empty and it would remain so until later that day when the arrival of his parents would bring about a questioning fear pertaining to the lack of his presence.

Mr. Michaels looked like an old man, but his true age might have surprised Doug. He had a mordacious grimace on his rubicund face when he inspected Doug's character as he entered.

His office was huge, and very refined. He was one of the seven directors of the whole dome. His desk was nicely carved and seemed to imitate the Chippendale style of the eighteenth century. It was characterized by a graceful outline engulfed by a baroque rococo ornamentation.

The back wall of this office was covered which a similar style of wood shaped into squares whose purpose was to hold wine. He had many alcoholic drinks there many of which were fine wines. On the other side he had some beers including bock.

The wall with the wine was so different from the others in their promotion of a business atmosphere that its distinction enraptured Doug. If he didn't look anywhere else, and only stared at the wine he could have imagined himself in some bodega or winery with the man on his other side as Dionysus, the God of wine.

Not only did it seem out of place there, but Doug thought that it wasn't allowed in the workplace. With power came freedom.

Mr. Michaels seeing Doug's scrutinizing glances provided an answer, "My hobby."

They spoke for some time, and the job offer indeed lived up to Doug's expectations. One of the details, however, he didn't like. He would be located in the same building in which Andrew resided.

Did this come about by chance? Did Andrew intend for Doug to meet Susi, and somehow lure him over to his dome? Maybe Mr. Michaels worked for him and they were already on to Alan's change of identity. In any event, Doug had to make the best decision. He acted under the assumption that no one knew of Alan's presence, and turned down the submission.

He wasn't an adult. Maybe he wanted some of the child-like imagination that presented this world as a game to him. At the same time he also knew that it was very serious, but he couldn't resist playing with various ideas and possibilities as if his life were some adventure.

He walked out of the office a gentleman. He was always nice to the man, but he exercised the discretion, poise and tact for which the situation asked. He told him that he needed to continue disciplining and educating himself for some time before he was ready for a job. The man understood. Doug felt that he handled it all perfectly. For the first time he didn't rely on his parents to give him advice, and he followed a part of his intuition that wasn't affected by the chimerical thoughts according to which he had formerly lived his life.

Susi wasn't angry when he entered the old lab fifteen minutes late.

They spoke of their lives and what they had missed telling each other when they had been separated by a stretch of necessity. They promised each other that they would never be distanced again.

Susi's shriek echoed within the encasement of the unused metal machinery. She looked up, and then the next time she saw him, he just lye in front of her with a cold stare unable to perceive anything. He was unconscious.

An old hefty computer monitor fell from a height of about fifteen feet causing blood to trickle down onto the brown tiled floor, and causing him to be unreceptive of anything after it struck him.

He couldn't have predicted this when just a few seconds earlier he moved over some crates in the dark room and sauntered over to a stack of boxes upon which he wanted to sit. A freak accident can occur anywhere at anytime, but Doug wasn't thinking of this as he nudged a broken mass spectrometer at the base of a pile of rubble dislodging the computer monitor at the top.

❖ *Chapter Twenty-one* ❖

A butterfly uses the wind, gracefully, to glide to a destination. It lives twice and captures two different perspectives on life each time it is born. The first birth comes as a shock. Out of nothing it is given a life. It has to live out this existence as it will later recollect as an ugly form blindly following the cravings that its parasitic frame demands by feeding on anything of its liking. This is the limit of its first life. It has an appetite, and a limited view of its environment since it only has the ability to inch towards the leaves for which its lust creates a blind obligation. There isn't any other interest or ability to see anything else. This mere existence is sustained not because of a hope for something more agreeable or pleasing, but because there is no way out. And so it sets up the most favorable conditions for itself by doing the most that it can within its limited field of view unconsciously giving substance to its second birth. In its cocoon it lies in dormancy escaping the life that it didn't understand or want to be a part of anymore, and emerges as something completely different. It isn't hard-featured or offensive anymore because it doesn't see the world that way. The vision in the air offers it all of beauty that it didn't have time to see before, and this beauty ascertains the boundaries of its inner beauty which shows up on the outer and newly enhanced frame. This life may also not be understood just as the previous one wasn't, but the attractiveness and freedom of this aerialist is compelling enough to continue existence just for the delight it has to offer. For it, this is the second beginning; the second genesis.

Without forewarning it is all taken away. An unusual breeze caused by a huge object, which barely misses it, forces it to give up its occasional gliding. It strains in vain, void of any assistance, to preserve its position so that it isn't pulled into the air vortex following the object's trajectory. Upon its impact near a durmast oak, the sound of fear penetrates the ears of all who listen. No one could escape the sound for it reaches even the ears most unwilling to listen. The butterfly burns up in what seems like a millisecond without even giving any natural sensor in it the chance to be apprised by danger. No warning. No feeling. It is an all too easy passage away from beauty.

*   *   *

Another impact far away from the first one caused the lights to flicker in Alan's abode waking him up. The ground shook ever so slightly. This wasn't too unusual. It shook before when construction was underway. He casually moseyed into Doug's room, seeing no need for alarm, where Doug felt secure under his blanket just like a child would.

There was another tremble. This one much bigger in magnitude than its predecessor. Never before had anything been felt like this. Articles of clothing fell off a nearby rack, the archaic trombone which Alan had bought to quench Doug's incredible thirst for history for his nineteenth birthday fell off the pillow Doug had lain it on, all of the experimental computer chips which Alan had brought home fell onto the carpet and succumbed to disorder, and every small unfastened object fell to a more stable position of equilibrium. The glasses in the kitchen shook like all the bottles of wine in Mr. Michaels office which he poorly fastened in the elegance that helped further the eventual mass destruction of each one of them. Now alarm arose, and there was need for it!

Everything was topsy-turvy. Liz, who had sent Allan to comfort Doug and Rob during the first unwelcome awakening, found herself out of bed running towards Doug's room.

In the halls outside their impervious security door, people shrieked and ran as if they could somehow escape the effects they felt caused by the undiscovered source. The deployment sound of one-man shuttles presented Alan and his family with a continuous pitch that wouldn't die down, making them believe that there was an endless line of those shuttles. The tone sounded like that of the unheard fear-invoking "thump" that never reached the butterfly or any human in a ten meter radius on the ground above.

Liz answered the door only to find Susi in panic.

Outside the dome itself, beyond the security of water, topsy-turvy made its meaning known to everyone. A few minutes ago cruisers had flown through the air as if they were made of paper, and people disintegrated before being able to yell to loved ones. Whole building vanished, leaving piles of burning rubble behind. Many plants, animals, humans, and other life forms had disappeared from this planet and the last feeling and mood that stayed in the rubble left behind between the dead and the dying expressed to the survivors miles away from ground zero the feelings of fear, alarm, and concern rooted in the curiosity which these departed people had felt.

This was many times worse than the so called "Epoch of Pandemonium" that plagued some of the veterans who were able to experience a much greater magnitude of their past again.

Once again, the sky turned black and blocked out the sun for what the survivors thought would be years. They saw the darkness but they didn't have time to think of its repercussion. Sunlight seemed as a visitor would to the land; it could be pushed away any time it wasn't welcome. It wasn't like the light that was let into Alan's closet under the hands of his captors: unyielding, unstoppable, all encompassing. This was an expatriate living in a foreign land, unable to reconcile with its inability to retain its reign of almost faultless attendance.

Those that happened to be in underground retreats didn't have much to return to when the fires died down. The cost of rebuilding this would have been immeasurable.

Within an hour much land had been cleared. In some areas it looked like the Restricted Regions of the country: barren desert filled like a junkyard with scraps of metal, and ignescent plastic, and wood that had had been set ablaze creating the foreboding darkness.

The floating Refueling and Resting Dock directly above the HYI8764653 TERRITORY received an extra but unwanted lagniappe by mishap from the wicked hand that unleashed this terror. Two implosions occurred right next to each other no farther than two miles apart. One was an air burst to the left of the refueling station, and the other was a sub-surface burst in the water to its right. The two resulting shock waves, seen as a moving wall of highly compressed air, converged and collided directly at the location of this floating platform, skyrocketing it with a high velocity upward.

The small hydrofoils that were docked in the small anchorage weren't given the opportunity to follow the platform station into the sky. They fell apart as if they had been made of toothpicks the instant they experienced the simultaneity of the two high-pressure waves. All that was left were a few pieces of floating rubber enough for a distant observer to mistaken them for simple johnboats. The waves eventually passed through each other returning to their initial size, but not before creating a maximum amplitude of the sum of the their individual amplitudes at the colliding moment.

The subsurface burst caused a huge explosion five territories away from Doug's location which caused the tremble and power outage they had felt. Close to one of the shrouded and concealed hydro-metallurgy labs there was a storage area for lyddite, a high explosive composed chiefly of picric acid. The wave disrupted some of the functioning machinery and molten lead was poured onto the ground igniting everything that it touched. It wasn't long before it reached the lyddite.

The war had begun. No one knew how—they just ran for their lives from an undeniable ending. The blasts killed many, but it was the aftereffects of the fusillade that hurt many more. There were strong winds associate with the passage of the blast wave. These winds had a peak velocity of several hundred miles per hour near ground zero. The overpressure, the pressure in excess of the normal atmospheric pressure, and these winds were the major contributors to the casualty and damage-producing effects of the nuclear outburst.

About one minute after the first burst, when the fireball was no longer visible, the blast wave traveled about forty miles and still moved slightly faster than the speed of sound.

Businessmen one-hundred and five miles away, saw the fireball of the explosion of this one megaton weapon many times more brilliant than the Sun at noon. Many were permanently blinded because of the cloudy conditions that served to emphasize this great coruscating and bright distinction in the environment.

The individual shuttles that came to the surface never made it back down to the lab which they never realized was their only shelter.

Man had gotten his wish or at least thought that he had. He invaded nature and replaced it with one that was more temperate to his liking. In his attempt to surmount it, he only eliminated his existence. He restrained it by imposing agony upon it, but this only temporarily injured, the absolute nature which could never go away.

Now people faced the tools of amelioration and improvement that they had created. The reformers that guided the tools' progress came in the form of the low penetrating alpha, the high-speed electron beta, and the shorter wavelength higher energy gamma radiation. The unit of the roentgen formed the scale upon which this new science tried to vaingloriously but unavailing measure success. This scale covered the agony of superiority for which an exposure to six hundred or more roentgens was deemed a complete success while one of fifty to two hundred roentgens implied a stronger need for science to further new creations which were to dwindle the rate of survival abolishing any need for life or love.

❖ *Chapter Twenty-two* ❖

Darkness is all that they saw and would see for a while. Who knew how long they would have to suffer? They couldn't answer that question because they didn't have a destination. They lost two homes, and the third brought all of their insecurity back to haunt them.

Water was leaking in from all sides. The emergency doors were closed in some sectors of the dome, and the people trapped between them never got out. They drowned so that the others could get a chance to live. The explosion had caused an earthquake which had disrupted much of the structural integrity of the dome. Alan rushed through the hall knee deep in water. It was difficult to run because he had to step over debris and bodies, but he made it through the electronic gate just before it closed off access from the old abode containing his only possessions.

They were in an intersection that had two exits closed. Neither of them knew which way to go.

Trying to find some signs of the hope or compassion she had seen expressed before in the eyes of her precious husband who loved her beyond belief, Liz gripped his hand tightly. It didn't help though because his love for her couldn't tell him what to do. He hadn't even known what had happened.

Susi was hysterical, and cried in Doug's arms while he felt like doing the same.

If they were all to die right on this spot and if he had to accept it, though, he wouldn't feel an appropriate closure to the lives of his family or his own life. He was as lost as them, but he knew why Liz had married him years ago. It was because of his determined nature that he always tried to make the best out of every situation for he never let the elements in life to trouble him. Liz married him because he had courage to face the most discouraging incidents and never once seriously complained about his life. If he did complain it was over the simple things that Liz knew he didn't take seriously. Now she needed him for the defender and protector his inner confidence expressed to her on the outside. He didn't show the fear on his face as she did. He concealed it very

154

well as he did throughout his life. He did it so many times that he wasn't so sure that he could be afraid. What he did express was a persistence consequent of a firmness of mind to rescue the children which his wife had wanted to carry on the traits she admired so much in his being.

He showed that his hesitation was not from anxiety, but from concern for his family's welfare as he made a bold and self-assured step that turned into a brisk run down the southbound tunnel. They ran for some distance until they came to the Tunnel Rail. It obviously wasn't running since the rising water level indicated that somewhere along the line a leak had sprung. It did lead, though, to another dome in which they could be safe.

There were a few people running around in the commotion just as confused as they themselves were. Some panicked so much that they looked like they were going to die without anything even hurting them.

A man was running down to the same tunnel probably with a similar idea. It was Warren. He had worked with Alan before on a project dedicated to investigating and probing Jupiter's moon, IO.

His words barley reached Alan through the noise from the machinery, the siren and the people.

"Alan! I never expected to see you again!"

"Likewise!"

"Follow me we must go to the Development Lab."

Alan didn't want to. His plan was to find a small shuttle that could take him to the ground. He let Warren know very simply just by not following him.

"Alan we have no other choice."

"Why?"

"I was monitoring the Refueling Dock above us during the arrival of the prime minister today. There were nuclear detonations. I don't know how many. We got to go now before we drown."

Alan missed much of what Warren said, but he heard all that he needed for him to act.

The Development Lab was sealed, being one of many that was restricted. The quick slide of Warren's key moved the massive steel doors. They took the N.W.C. (nuclear waste carrier) which was empty at the time. It was used to carry toxic wastes to the depths of the ocean were it was deposited into strong and durable plastic-type material.

There was silence and then the sound that for the time being eased their misery and bewilderment—the dampened noise of expulsion as the pod backfired and released itself from the firm grip of destruction.

They all looked back from the small globular glass lunette and saw a divergence of reality as they were able to observe the lovely structure they had been living in for the past year from the outside. The farther out they got, the more it looked like an image from a dream. The lights which had turned on in the dome enhanced this effect. It was pitch black. This was somewhat normal for the depth that they were at, but something was definitely missing. Normally, even at these depths, nature's lighting could be felt. Today this feeling was absent.

"Where are you going!"

He looked at Alan. "I told you. We can't emerge. The radiation would kill us."

Warren let the ship move, and occasionally nudged it by following some dots on a computer screen. The red dot was the pod. The blue one was what they were approaching. Every time he tapped the steering it would realign its course with the blue dot.

He looked at Susi, Doug, and Rob. "Whatever they used, they weren't A-bombs. These were much more potent."

They descended farther into the depths and entered a dome concealed by a canyon on the ocean floor. It was camouflaged so perfectly that Alan first asked why they had gone there.

Warren told them about the proposal V.O.R.T.E.X. with which they both had worked. Alan had forgotten much about it. He thought the idea had been dismissed since someone had told him that it would have cost NAST billions of dollars.

Upon entering a dark gorge, they turned slightly upward as if they were going to make a "U" turn and found themselves floating above in a small pool of water surrounded by walls on each side. A voice from a speaker at the top of the open pit called out and Warren answered, stating that this was an emergency. A few more words were exchanged.

The walls fell down and all of them were surrounded my about ten armed men who extensively checked the visitors.

A few hours had passed.

Doug saw the inscribed letters "V.O.R.T.E.X." above a doorway. As he walked through it he was confounded. Susi's reaction was the same. Never before had they seen anything like this. The monstrous room they entered was bigger than ten warehouses. It was like an indoor coliseum only bigger. The distance to the ceiling of this area was almost the same as its length.

In front of him was a metal aircraft. Another three just like it were located at different areas in the ocean floor. All the way in the back of this mighty ship were two half moons curving around the body. It had lights all over and plastic windows in the front and on the sides. There were long pieces of metal sticking out of one side that looked like double barrel automatic aircraft guns or Bofor guns.

Doug was observing this from an upper platform. He had to walk over to his extreme right to get a closer look. Each rod seemed to have a barbette around it just as a cylinder of armor would protect a gun turret on a warship.

When he ran around the whole platform, which seemed like a giant upper track, he saw that the other side of the ship had the same structure. It was fantastic. He could have stared forever at it, observing all the little gadgets on the outside. He left the job of making up what the insides looked like to his imagination. How he wished that he could sneak in just to satisfy his urges of interest!

Contrary to Alan's beliefs, the project had been underway for many years now. He thought that it had ended because that is what NAST wanted him to believe. This ship was too important to let average people work with it, and to hold its future in their hands. It became a top secret priority to withhold any information concerning its existence because the energy needed for its warp engines was based on the applied fusion technology that NAST wanted to keep dormant.

It was a ship capable of carrying one hundred people for a twenty year mission. It contained 7.9 million pounds of water, 3.3 million pounds of food, and 1.1 million pounds of oxygen. It could attain a maximum speed of half the speed of light: one hundred and twenty million meters per second. The radiation emitted by the engines at these high speeds was secluded from the passengers by an absorptive barrier. In addition, the ship was designed to accelerate within the range of human tolerance.

Doug and Susi stood fixed in a trance as they took in the complexity of what lay before them.

Alan and the others went in another room to establish communication with some other parts of the territory. It was useless, though.

A satellite radar that showed all parts of the world along with their weather patterns revealed a disturbing truth.

The United States had been destroyed by an enemy bold enough to use efficacious weapons, but insensate enough not to understand what the possible effects could be.

The ignorance provoked an act of further feeble-mindedness as the United States between the successive attacks it received launched what was considered by many as the greatest defensive weapon on earth. It was based on the fusion bomb that used a fission type of explosion to generate the needed energy to fuse the atoms of a material contained within it. This would release a second amount of tremendous energy much more spectacular than the first. This bomb had many more times the power of a hydrogen bomb, but it was purely a shielding weapon. This was emphasized by its creators, and it was to be used under the worst circumstances.

There have been many riots aimed at the government by concerned citizens whose good aim was the abolishment of this one weapon because it had the potential to destroy the globe. They were right.

The US kept it because many countries were starving, lacking fossil fuels, and polluted without having the technology they needed to clean up. Poverty and extermination could bring out much hate, especially towards the group that had the most and seemed responsible for all the scarcity. That was why the weapon was kept. If exploitation, which brought about inequality, was the motto that was lived by before then it was time for it to move on to new heights where it could tally with destruction.

So it was released, perhaps by accident, one month before its intended dismantling. The riots finally won over the minds of the people who had been corrupted by the fictitious ideals of the evolution of exploitation because they convinced them that the effects of such a weapon couldn't be known for certain unless it was tested. They were to make sure that it wouldn't be tested. Their efforts, though, produced an action that never arrived. One month made a world of difference. One month determined the future.

The detailed satellite images showed repeatedly picture after picture how every region was blackened meaning that the radiation had spread everywhere. Russia, the target itself, was gone. No longer could it be considered to be on a map.

The whole world felt the effects of some conflict that could be nothing but petty when contrasted with the massive depopulation and genocide of the world's inhabitants. Without knowing what had happened, some in the poverty stricken regions without access to communication believed that the predictions of a meteoric strike upon the earth had come true.

The lasting wreckage and rubble thrown into the air which blocked out the sun would have killed the vegetation that animals needed to grow and humans needed to survive. Those that survived the radiation would have to face the poverty which would be extended from the exploited countries to everyone.

The slow battle against the earth that man began had suddenly been accelerated not giving way to any merciless cries. There were no other options.

The dome resting above them on the underwater peak from where they came was loosened and pieces of rock and mud that slipped down to the facility they now were in indicated another coming disaster. The explosion cut off the dome from the Tunnel Rail that had held it like a string above the abyss. It tumbled. It impacted. Water rushed in and around Doug once again.

As the engines became engilded and steam rose from the warehouse water soaked floor which the engines tried hopelessly to exsiccate, Doug felt blood rush from his head just as he had in the past when he had gotten into an accident with the cruiser before he went to the so called graduation party. When the cruiser first escaped his control, he felt as if it weren't happening. How could it? It was such a different experience from common livelihood that no history exists which informs thoughts about how to translate emotions of concern into action.

He felt the same here. It couldn't be happening. He got dizzy, and fainted.

Susi went into shock.

Liz also felt the dizziness. She associated this with the feelings she had had when her mother had passed away. They were deviant from the way she expected life to be. Her daily life up till now served as a reminder of her dreams which sometimes told her that her mother was still alive. She would go on with those thoughts for some time because she became used to them. Only after questioning them would she come to the truth. The same occurred now, except that she didn't dream. She didn't think that this wasn't happening. She didn't have the time because she experienced ever horror stricken second of it, and there was no way of releasing the squeeze that it had on her mentality. She couldn't go anywhere or do anything except confront everything presented to her with a judgment, when her mind was clear enough to do so.

No one knew what Alan was thinking nor did they ask.

They weren't ready to depart. They had their arms around each other maintaining a circle and wishing that death could come quickly, not so much because they were afraid of it, but because they feared the terror that would be left with the loved ones next to them if they had an inadequate and disagreeable death.

❖ *Chapter Twenty-three* ❖

It was over for it, but it still retained its dazzling appearance from above. Pictures often portrayed the Earth with a whitish light surrounding its circumference that made it distinct from the blackness of space in which it was imbibed. Those pictures didn't lie. The Earth did have a force field that guaranteed life; an ambiance which showed every living creature the marvelous world in which it lived.

They broke through the surface of the ocean on which they traveled for some time to get to land. To get out of the Earth's gravitational pull, they needed a surface launch. They were to get a first hand look at the destruction they first saw on the satellite images. Then there was the launch. A stretch of level ground set them on their way. A hullabaloo . . . the engines strained and during the next few seconds they were in the lowest region of the atmosphere: the troposphere.

From the stratosphere a part of the Earth's form was taking shape. The Earth was in its transformation into a sun. It seemed as if the interior wanted to release heat and light that it had been holding. Many solar flares had broken out all over the surface. This is the effect that man had on it.

Finally out of its gravitational pull the force field could be seen. Under these present conditions though, the field was a different color. Life wasn't protected by the usual brightness anymore. In some areas it was just black. In others the field looked empurpled. The color changed its purpose. Nuclear technology caused it to hold an enmity towards the land that betrayed it. Alan was the only one partially conscious of this vision that he saw out of the small windows.

They embarked on this voyage when the moon was in its interlunar stage. Never again would they see the interval between their old and new moon.

Doug lived as they all did: one day at a time. It wasn't easy to predict what would happen next. He woke up wondering if he would survive the next day.

They had a mission. Every one of the two hundred and seventy three people on the three ships that exited the home they were born and raised on had a mission. They had to sustain and preserve the human race. The objective was to find some habitat suitable for sustaining life.

This goal seemed as ridiculous to Doug as anyone else, but the starting engines of this new gigantic moving dome of detention proved to show that there was no other option.

One suggestion was to spend twenty years in space close to Earth to let the environment regenerate. This was dismissed because the radiation from this weapon had a half life of two hundred years.

The synthetic element, Ve, discovered five years ago which was used to build this bomb produced an unimaginable reaction when exposed to oxygen in any form, be it that of the atmosphere or of the water. Engineers formed it in a synthetic substance mixed with oil. The bomb's explosion allowed Ve to breathe for the first time. Its exposure to oxygen formed new Ve in the air which reacted with more oxygen and produced more toxins. It was an unstoppable chain reaction. A jar of oil no bigger than a fist contained a vile substance which destroyed everything. No one could have guessed that it could have had such a colossal effect on humanity!

When scientists first detonated the first A-bomb they had a fear that the atmosphere would explode and produce a similar effect as that of Ve. Their successful bidding on the world's future proved tempting enough to try it again, only this time they lost.

The ship couldn't come back because there wouldn't be any life around waiting for their arrival. Also, there wasn't enough of a time dilation to return after traveling ten or twenty years to an Earth that has aged more than two hundred. At their speed, they would only aged eighteen years for a given twenty year Earth period.

The next closest star to Earth was Alpha Centauri which was about four light years away. It could be probable that some life could exist in its vicinity. The chances that the life there would accommodate the human body were one in a billion. Many saw this voyage as a diagnosis for a twenty year life. They didn't expect to live any longer.

Depression settled in on the ship. People's faces showed the inner hopelessness they were feeling. A few committed suicide. The others weren't so daring or lurdane. They wanted to put up a struggle. There was always time for death later.

Doug looked outside his triple glass window protected from the abstruse world. Was it better to see nothing than to see ocean water as he had in the undersea lab? There were only a few glimmering lights enveloped by the darkness, but those that he saw provided little comfort. They looked too small to believe that life could ever exist in their vicinity. Recalling the events of his life building up to the posterity of which he didn't want to be a part of, didn't help resolve his dubious future. Doug wondered if it had all been somehow intended. If all the sacrifices that were made gave room for some outer development. He couldn't think of what was still to come so he spent his energy on remembering the elapsed days of his disconsolate life. He could have been different.

He could have treated others differently. He spent most of his youth trying to fit in with others; caring too much about what they thought. He has acted confidently when he wanted to, but only to have pleased others. He wasn't happy with himself, then, and it hurt him to think that he wasted a happiness to which he was entitled.

Since Herbert showed him the way, he did much thinking. Now he felt better even though his life was over. He lost the fear that he had before the ship had taken off, and he felt at peace with himself because he only lived in the moment. He lost all resentment. Eighty percent of is old thoughts focused on the past, but now he didn't think of it at all. Consequently, his actions changed. He loved and approved of himself and others around him.

His change in personality took time. It was like a marble held onto the side wall of a concave up bowl. At the top of the bowl his ego and superficial needs reigned supreme. At the bottom, his ego was powerless. A deeper part of his being took control there. During the transition to his desired personality which was free from worries, Doug fell like the marble. He slipped towards the bottom of the bowl and climbed the edges a few times before he was stable and rested on the bottom. This irregular motion, resembling a damped simple harmonic motion or oscillation, expressed itself in the way he acted. When the marble was on the wall, he felt the need for slight arrogance. As the marble gained height on the other side, his greed increased. The marble, however, always lost energy on the opposite side. So his maximum arrogance and lack of compassion on a given day was always less than the maximum attained in the past just after passing the point of equilibrium and love.

This created the fluctuations in his emotions. The bowl of emptiness now provided a friction which made him clearly see his goal.

He was sure that now he was very close to the bottom of the bowl. The marble only gained a slight height on the edges of his ego, and it spent much of its time in the spiritual part of his sphere of being.

He knew that his determination and inquisitive mind led him to this happiness.

With every new day he felt better and better about himself. He had to give this feeling to everybody around him so that at least they could die in peace. It didn't matter if he had twenty years to live as long as he proved consistent in this higher level of meditative-like consciousness.

Outside the window, the chartreuse color from the outside lights, that emanated from their centers, meant something different for him than anybody else. For others, it meant a hopeless view and acceleration into nonexistence. Whether the light shined or not didn't matter. When it would disappear they would glide at constant speed towards an unfavorable destination. For Doug, the variable color averaging a brilliant yellow-green set a time limit. Once extinguished, resources will be depleting. He had the other half of his life left to bring people to the enlightened state of mind that the first half of his curiosity-filled existence gave him.

He couldn't doubt that the mystery of space was beautiful. If only this could be a vacation, he would be loving it. He still saw the moon in his mind as he had seen it when they passed by.

For a long time there was nothing only blackness.

Man had found the final challenge, but could he successfully beat its vastness? Before the goal was to cross an ocean to discover America, and other new lands. Space was another step forward, but it was too complex to understand or discover fully. Even with time, technology couldn't unleash the secrets that it held.

Doug had thought that it would have been beautiful to travel the universe; to explore and make new discoveries about the unknown. It was a dream to work for NAST and lead distant explorations of the planets. Now space seemed dull and frightening. It contained many things that were yet to be discovered but that didn't seem to matter as much anymore. Man had much technology. He didn't need more, except for the discoveries that came along the way, but man didn't have to focus all of his energies on this advancement. Doug knew that Einstein was right when he said that man's technology had surpassed his humanity.

As Doug remembered the picture of the Earth he knew that that was the place where man should have done some exploration. Many advancements were still needed, but it was the technology which had to be put aside. The seemingly small globe stood out from the blackness in which there was nothing. Man's place was on earth, and that was where he should have stayed. He didn't need to explore given the gargantuan possession he started out with.

He received the same ration that he got every day. It was nothing fancy. To tell the truth it sickened him to imagine that besides the dunnage in the cargo area (a great percentage of the ship) was this tasteless larder. It was very plain. Of course he would have rather relished some fine Dunlop or cisco, but this was said to be full of nutrients.

He ate and meditated again. It was easy to leave his body this time. As long as he focused on something—anything, he would alter his perception of reality. It felt good.

He didn't quite know what was happening to him, and he couldn't really describe the experience to anyone because it was so extreme and queer, it was beyond explanation. It just felt good, but it was like seeing a gold mine only to have it sink to the depths of the ocean before others are told about it. Words would have promoted disbelief until visual authentication could have been produced by each separate individual. Given this criteria, twenty years was just about the right length of time.

He changed his mantra: "I feel powerful and alive I couldn't care if the world dies." This saying was driven by the ego he wanted removed from every facet of his life. He didn't need to concentrate on being unsound and regretful. He now knew what he wanted. His new mantra was simple and meaningless, yet he thought of love while saying it.

This was the reason to live. The next twenty years would be a new beginning for him, and he just discovered the beauty in them even if no one else saw it. His resolve, tenacity, and determination finally made him stumble, willingly, upon the undiscovered beauty of genesis. He felt every part of his entirety gaining a fullness and completion.

There was peace; an absence of noise. Herbert came up to him. He handed him a translation of *Nevesta Kristova*:

> *O God! Good Shepherd protect the honest people, change sinners, be kind to the poor, less fortunate, sick, weak, dying, the dead, and those who died. Be compassionate to me poor sinner. Amen.*

It was a prayer from an ancient bible! The relief that came from knowing this was less than the relief of knowing what to do with it. He would use it to bring happiness to the people who have given up.

Herbert then spoke in a monotonous voice. "Three weeks before the ship was launched, Andrew, your father's old boss, held a meeting two domes away from where you used to live in room three fifty-six. After the meeting he sold highly secretive information about the fusion project to Russia. Originally it was meant for the leaders of the Unified Asian and European communities who would keep this information to themselves instead of sharing it. They desperately needed energy to revive their countries' poverty. Andrew got a better offer from Russia and sold them the laboratory materials that would make cold fusion successful. The leaders of unified Asian and European communities got enraged and desperate. They sent a fleet of long range nuclear missiles to American soil with a screening device that indicated their origin was from Russian soil. Many thought that the war that ended years ago had begun all over again. Some of the missiles were intercepted, but the sheer numbers presented the US military with a situation they couldn't cope with.

They retaliated and destroyed Russia, and the true enemies that obscurely started the battle including everything else."

"The initiators that created the conflict saw it as a necessary step for survival. They either were to get the energy to help fight overpopulation in their countries or they were to provoke a fight which immediately depopulated two immense countries giving the world enough room to breathe once more and providing enough resources for everyone. No one expected this outcome. It was the fault of one man."

Herbert told him more. He gave him details. Doug questioned them. Why did he mention them? How had he known this? How did he get on the ship?

❖ *Chapter Twenty-four* ❖

Doug woke up. He saw them again. The way that he tried to remember them when he departed. Susi, and his mother were sitting by his bed on a bench. They kept busy with, what from his perspective looked like, an active discussion. He was staring right at them when Susi, who was facing him, stared back forcing his mother to turn around. There was a scream and he was hugged and cried for. He didn't quite know why.

Two weeks were a long time. A fortnight of his present life looked good when compared to the fortnight of hell. He wouldn't ever want to go away again. He was happy just where he was. According to his reasoning, and the details that Herbert spoke of, he had one week to make sure that he wouldn't have to relive the fortnight that took him away from the presently high spirits of the people he loved.

His father and brother ran in as soon as they heard of the miracle. They all almost sent him off to another voyage of deep sleep as they crowded around his bed suffocating him with their affection and euphoria.

Doug woke up from his coma. The abrupt transition startled him, and he almost passed out. At first he had to think where he was, and he had to gain the memory that he had almost lost due to confusion he had *lived*. When he did remember he felt relieved that the monitor hit him, but he was too weak to discuss the future visions he had seen.

Three days passed. Doug felt strong enough to get up. He couldn't sleep any longer.

He was convinced that he saw the future and during the exact interval of time which he spent lying in bed he was experiencing a very different life. He knew that it was real. He was afraid to tell anyone because they might have thought that he hadn't come out of this accident with his old mental health intact. So he kept it a secret and waited.

Maybe his family would have been correct to assume that he had made it up. Perhaps meditation had altered his mind too much. He decided to

166

test these slight doubts by confirming the many predictions he received. One of them was the room number that in a few days Andrew should hold a meeting in. The exact location was told to Doug, along with a description of the room, the number of people in it, the clothes that Andrew would be wearing, the number of guards outside, and much more. The guards where there because this meeting was held in a secret facility in the heart of the fusion laboratory.

When the time came Doug tested the truth of the future he knew he had experienced.

He sneaked out of bed and walked down the hall which he last remembered as slowly being filled with water. The reality he was a part of now was just as real as before. Was there a difference between the two? Will he wake up again somewhere only to doubt that he should really be there?

He calmly walked into his room. He got dressed into appropriate apparel, and walked to the Tunnel Rail.

One . . . Two . . . Three, he passed these domes faster than he thought he would. At the fourth dome, security checked everyone that got off so before he reached it, he pushed the emergency button, pulled the sliding window on the side next to his seat and jumped out onto an upper rail used by construction workers. He sat in the back of the Transport so no one saw him do this.

As he walked on the rail, he passed a room with many boxes and an officer in it stacking them on top of each other. This was exactly the situation as described by Herbert. As a matter of fact everything he did and was going to do followed the indirect instructions he received. He felt so hardened by what he had already seen and heard that he felt nothing stopping his hand as it reached for the officers stun gun, and pressed it up against his jacket. The shocked man turned abruptly to see him just before he collapsed.

He went through the storage area and into the main complex with this weapon and a particle gun he also obtained.

He stunned three more officers that he met along the hallways always getting close enough by pretending to be lost. He knew that he didn't have much time because the security cameras already spotted him.

As he turned a corner through the guided maze he saw the outline of a man at the distant end of it whom he knew to be Andrew. He was sure that he was headed into room three fifty-six.

All that Doug saw as the man walked out of view was the partial reflection of light from his shiny clothes and his outlying facial features of which the large snout that he had to muzzle, was the most distinctive.

Every clue anticipated and foreseen had come true.

Doug knew that Andrew killed Luke and many more almost including his father among his sacrificial victims whose souls he took to improve his own glory.

He may have appeared impeccable to others in the business world who were oblivious to his true identity, but Doug knew better. He couldn't hide knowing this. The insight into global improvement lighted the path towards his confrontation.

Doug had to swear Andrew into the sphere of being his disposition would most appreciate. He raced down the second hall to reach the room where Andrew's inauguration was to take place. As he ran he felt like Andrew was the game here and he tracked him down with the hounds of enlightenment. The short coursing was underway.

The name of Doug's emulator rang in his ears as he yelled it out at the top of his lungs.

He just entered the room when he noticed a group of ten fashionably dressed people who looked at him—the psychotomimetic individual standing in a facility which he had no right to be in. Towering above those gazes was Andrew's own cold gaze. His leering eyes tried to enhance the contretemp that he thought Doug was already feeling.

"What is it son?"

Andrew thought that he would present Doug with the topmost embarrassment he could by showing him how out of place he really was. Even though he didn't know the boy, he intended to make this situation into an entertaining moment. "Are you lost?"

Just before the marble stuck the resting equilibrium at the bottom of the bowl of life it weakly tried to climb the walls of insecurity a little bit for one last time. Doug felt slightly uneasy. Instead of a hunter he had become a passive plant growing in the darkness, extending his arms for a light that he couldn't find. He knew that he would eventually die if he didn't find the light.

Andrew, having the upper hand, didn't need to be the game anymore. His powerful gaze seemed to emit toxins into the air subduing the energy Doug had felt when he entered the room. He couldn't be suppressed. He wouldn't give in to Andrew's allelopathic hold on his freedom.

"Well what do you want?"

"Forgiveness for Luke, and many others that died because of your strangling hold on their lives."

What he said after that didn't matter. He could have denied it. He could have laughed. He knew the truth which Doug spoke of and nothing else mattered. He didn't need any circumstantiation to expiate the dead.

Doug heard the footsteps and yelling voices of many officers as they ran down the hall.

Doug withdrew the particle gun. He felt ease and enlightenment for a final and lasting time as the marble rested at the bottom of the bowl. He pointed it at Andrew. He could hear the singing voices of billions of people. Andrew doddered as he was hit in the leg. He saw a collage of animals that have been saved and given the permission to live. Andrew fell as he received the final coup de grace from his personal arbiter. A lasting peace overtook the lives of the living and the posterity to come.

The advocate of bereavement was immolated for the future of love on Earth.

❖ *Chapter Twenty-five* ❖

He could see the sky. Despite all this he was still able to see beauty. Small clusters of clouds gathered and stuck together magnificently as melted marshmallows. They preferred to be together such that no lone clouds could be seen surrounded by the vast empty blue. He could have made objects out of them in his mind, but that might have resulted from boredom, anxiety, fear, or anger. He didn't have any need to distract his thoughts with the unnecessary occupation of these unimportant images.

A bit of redness crept into the pure blue. It started slowly from the East. Its main body was red, but its borders were scattered and spread out like thorns held in negligence growing in the wilderness, lacking sunlight. The frontier, joining the scattered redness to the whole, appeared like a fungus growing off and using the unprotected. Its efficacy produced undeserving feelings that his comfort humbly and almost unwilling accepted.

He was weary. He didn't think anymore. He didn't urge to meditate. The thorns urged him; they beckoned him to reach out to them and to feel them.

Hunger crept onto him, but now that he was able to suppress other thoughts he was able to control his hunger without fighting against this bodily desire. He remembered all that Herbert told him, all that Will told him, all that his parents told him, all that his friends told him, and even those words imparted to him indirectly by the psychic. Much of it wasn't relevant. It needlessly filled his mind, distracted his thoughts, and potential actions of goodness. It covered the truth creating an alias of untruth.

He knew he was going to live again. He knew this second life would last for eternity. Fear, greed, hatred, jealousy, anger, judgment, and distrust wouldn't be a part of him then. Now he had lived with these characteristics—in them, by them, for them, he worshipped only them—because he feared anything else. That was why he kept God at arms length all his life. The belief in himself and in his strength kept him alive avoiding the misery he felt only he could.

Now that he let his guard down and welcomed the misery, he really felt alive. Upon doing this, misery became a passion for joy.

Life had come to him.

Nothing anybody said mattered as much as what he now believed. His meditation brought out questions about himself that changed him and his free will accepted this change. He knew God existed. Even here in prison he felt something more powerful than urges for wealth or fame. It all came to him in the next few moments because he accepted it, and it loosely mixed in with the old life he didn't need anymore. Once he had lived in hatred. Doug felt all the judgments he imposed on people in the past disappear. Once he had lived in judgment. He was sorry for all the wrongs he had committed. Once he had lived in envy. He saw the superficial unimportance of many aspects of his present life. Once he had lived in untruth and deception. He desired forgiveness.

He reached the goal that his temporary stay on Earth was meant for. His life experience built up to this moment which was always there for him—he just refused to see it. He finally received the peace he never fully accepted or discovered until now.

❖ *Autobiography* ❖

I was born in New Jersey in 1978. I have been living in New Jersey all my life..

All through childhood, I have had an interest in the way that the human mind relates to itself and the world around it. I have had numerous interests which have tried to bring a fullness to the way I perceive the human spirit should interact with the community around it. My natural tendencies have led me to interests in sports, numerous hobbies, and clubs.

When I first attended the Newark Academy high school in Livingston I tried to continue the interests which have brought me the only type of satisfaction I ever experienced: a superficial satisfaction. I became involved in numerous clubs such as the Math Club, the Science Club, an executive of the Aids Awareness Club, president of the Chess Club, and an Amnesty International member. In addition I looked towards improving my physical definition by being a part of the track team for two years. I have enjoyed many of these experiences in that they taught me a way to improve personal qualities such as determination, leadership, and team work. Outside school, I became actively involved with HAM Radio. Despite these learning experiences and achievements, I still didn't feel that I was completing a part of myself that was crying out for attention.

As I began to understand this, I looked to a different path that would promote the expression of my individuality. With each subsequent English class throughout my four years at Newark Academy, my interests in literature and human identity grew. A more continual and almost desperate questioning of my environment has introduced me to a more specified branch of literature as I finished my high school experiences with a course in IB Philosophy.

Philosophy gave me insights, some of which related to my own personal beliefs, and I realized that this particular branch of study would give me my self the greatest gratification. I brought closure to my high school adventures with the James F. Manning Book Award in recognition of noteworthy growth in the ability to use the English language with perception and grace. I also took the International Baccalaureate exam in Philosophy on which I achieved an outstanding score. During my first year at Bucknell University in Pennsylvania I have continued to enjoy the elegance of the English language with a course in Creative Writing.

Overall, I received my B.S. degree in Chemical Engineering from Bucknell University and M.S. degree in Bioengineering from Penn State University. Since I wrote *The Undiscovered Beauty of Genesis*, I worked over two years at the pharmaceutical company Wyeth as a quality control scientist.

The experiences I have had, and the questioning of human individuality have inspired me to write *The Undiscovered Beauty of Genesis*. I hope that everyone will be able to attain and surpass the insights that their experiences in life have to offer them in order to gain a thorough understanding of the relationship between their expressions and the goal of their existence.